Aunt Daisy's Letter

by
S J Crabb

Copyrighted Material

Copyright © S J Crabb 2020

Contents

More books by S J Crabb

The Diary of Madison Brown

My Perfect Life at Cornish Cottage

My Christmas Boyfriend

Jetsetters

More from Life

A Special Kind of Advent

Fooling in love

Will You

Holly Island

sjcrabb.com

Quotes

"It does not do to dwell on dreams and forget to live." – J.K. Rowling

Enjoy the little things in life, for one day you may look back and realize they were the big things. ~Robert Breault

Twenty years from now you will be more disappointed by the things you didn't do than by the things you did. ~ Mark Twain

Somebody should tell us, right at the start of our lives, that we are dying. Then we might live life to the limit, every minute of every day. Do it! I say. Whatever you want to do, do it now! There are only so many tomorrows. ~ Pope Paul VI

Prologue

"Lily, are you in here?"

"Yes."

I look up as Aunt Daisy heads into the room. "There you are, what's going on?"

She looks around in surprise as I smile with satisfaction.

"Do you like it?"

She shakes her head slowly and then laughs. "You've done a good job; I certainly don't recognise the place."

Her praise is music to my ears because of all the members of my family, her words of encouragement mean the most because she is the successful one among us.

She sits and pats the space beside her. "Come and join me, darling, it's been ages since we caught up."

I do as she says with an eagerness to please, and as her arm curls around my shoulders, I settle into her side as I have many times before.

"You know, Lily, I see a lot of me in you."

I smile pleased with the comparison because if I had to be like anyone in life it would be her, you see, Aunt Daisy is beautiful, immaculately dressed and rich beyond any of our wildest dreams. She may be my father's sister, but somehow, she raced ahead in the race of life and started a business designing the homes of the rich and famous. She is good at it too and reaps the rewards, which is why I want to be just like her.

"I like what you've done, Lily, because it shows you have a creative flair. Develop it and then let it take you further than most people dare to dream exists. Take no prisoners and fly high above your peers because successful people don't let ordinary life get in the way. Fix your goals in place and when you reach them, set some more. Never stop striving for perfection because ultimately it will bring you great rewards. Don't let anyone drag you down to their level and run free with a spirit that cannot be contained."

She looks at me lovingly and her voice shakes a little as she says sadly, "If you find happiness, let it be on your own terms. Sometimes life throws a curved ball that only an expert can dodge. Be that expert, Lily, because it could knock you to the ground."

"What do you mean?" It all sounds a little confusing if I'm honest, and I'm not sure I understand the look in her eyes as she shakes her head and laughs softly. "Just be the best, Lily, don't settle for anything less and don't compromise your dreams for something you have no control over."

Looking around, she laughs. "I can see you have all the makings of a great designer yourself. I would never have thought of drawing such an intricate design on that wall over there and the colours you have used are bang on trend."

I look at the Art that I applied to the wall in her rather large bedroom proudly, as she ruffles my hair and giggles. "Maybe save it for the classroom though, I don't think your mum and dad would be quite as understanding if you decorated their walls in the same manner."

I look at her a little guiltily as she takes a tissue from the box by her bed and wipes the red lipstick I have smeared on my face away lightly.

"Let's get you cleaned up before they see your efforts." She winks and says in a whisper, "Let this be our little secret, darling. I won't tell if you won't."

As she leads me into her separate bathroom, I feel a surge of love for my pretty aunt.

Yes, when I grow up, I want to be just like Aunt Daisy. I am keen to start school on Monday just so I can finish it and be like her in every way.

Successful and rich. What more is there in life?

♥ 1

Twenty-five years later.

Thirty arrived like an unwelcome guest at my birthday party. I always knew it was coming and thought I had prepared myself mentally for the dawn of a new age, but when the dreaded day arrived, it brought with it a sinking feeling. So, that's it then. I've arrived at a turning point in my life and everything feels exactly the same.

The same wake-up call at 6am and the same sinking feeling as I contemplate the day ahead filled with nothing but work. Followed by a microwave meal for one in front of the television when I return to my bachelorette pad in the evening.

The same insecurities and panic attacks over the hoped-for promotion and the same lack of romance in my life. The same yearning for something better than I have already and the same face looking back at me in the mirror telling me, 'you should have done better.'

Then again, what did I expect? That suddenly the meaning of life would hit me and everything make sense. That I would see the glorious path of enlightenment lighting my way to a glittering new world, or maybe I would wake to the dawn of a brand-new era when everything that went before it made sense and the choices I made proved to be the right ones.

No, the only difference between waking up this morning and yesterday is the heavy heart that sits inside me because yesterday Aunt Daisy passed away.

As I make my usual cup of wake-me-up coffee, I think about the woman I aspired to be like in every way. My dad's sister and my godmother. She was beautiful, rich and successful. A woman of means as my father always described her with just a hint of envy in his voice. Where he had always struggled financially, she did not. Her house was the biggest our family had ever seen; her car was always new every three years and her holidays were to the most exotic locations, doing things the rest of us could only dream about. Yes, Aunt Daisy had it all, and the rest of us could just admire her for it.

When I heard she had died, I was in total shock. Apparently, she had a heart attack at home one night – in her sleep, and nobody knew until her cleaner found her two days later. You see, Aunt Daisy - like me - lived alone. She never married and that was how she wanted it – she told us often enough, and I never really thought much about it. She appeared to be happy with her life and who wouldn't?

I used to love going to visit. Unlike our rather dated semi-detached, her detached house was on a private road set among trees overlooking the golf course. Not that she ever played, of course. No, she was always too busy for hobbies. You see, she was a designer and her taste was bang on trend. Her company was successful as she designed the homes of the rich and famous and got paid extremely well for her trouble. Her staff was small but efficient, and her client base consisted of a few minor celebrities and people with way more money than sense. As expected, her own home was the stuff of dreams and any visit we made was spent coveting a lifestyle that set the bar high and made everyone wish they were her.

Now she's dead at fifty-five, and to say we are shocked is an understatement. She's gone and nobody saw it coming.

Sighing, I grab my coffee and set about getting ready for the daily commute to the office. Like Aunt Daisy, I was relentless in my pursuit of a career worth having. After university, I was lucky enough to land a job with the magazine of my dream and I worked my way up to become the impressive sounding junior editor of Designer Homes – *on a budget.*

I love my job and even my editor Sable Evans doesn't scare me half as much as she did when I started. Much like Aunt Daisy, Sable has life worked out and reaps the rewards. She is cold, calculating and professional, with none of the weaknesses the rest of us have to deal with on a daily basis. Sable power walks in every morning from the station instead of joining the queue for the underground. She exists on green tea and dubious looking smoothies, with only a rice cake for lunch. She dresses with an effortless chic and wears scarves that make her look stylish and elegant, unlike me who can't appear to tie them the right way and just gets flustered from dealing with the problems they bring. Like the time it got caught in the tube door and I spent the whole of the journey from Victoria to Green Park trying to free myself with my face pressed against the germ infested plasti-glass of the door. To add to my trauma, my fellow passengers took photos and videos and uploaded them to social media. I expect I'm still trending on Lad's Bible to this very day.

There was the time I decided to copy Sable and borrow one of Boris's bikes and cycle in through the rush hour traffic. After struggling to work out how to actually pay for the thing, I was extremely flustered and late when I set off, only for my scarf to get caught up in the spinning wheels and make me fall over sideways in the cycle lane in Piccadilly. I think that one made it onto the travel news as the congestion took all of two seconds to snarl up the West End, while I struggled to tear my chiffon fashion statement from the spokes of misery.

No, I haven't quite worked out the secret that Aunt Daisy and Sable were apparently born knowing, and I had kind of hoped that turning thirty would answer all those questions on auto pilot.

Sighing, I realise I'm just the same girl I always was. Lily Rose Adams. Named after two flowers because if one flower made Aunt Daisy successful, two would propel me to super success – or so they thought. Yes, I have spent the last thirty years being moulded into a carbon copy of the successful one in our family. Aunt Daisy was the perfect role model and I based every choice I made in life on what she would do.

To be fair, I've done the right thing, so far, anyway. I am *nearly* successful and, in my friend's eyes, have the perfect life. I'm sure it was like this for Aunt Daisy at the beginning and so, with a sigh, I dress for the day and start the first day of my thirties the same as the last day of my twenties. On a train bound for London and Designer Homes – *on a budget*.

♥ 2

Most of the journey is spent updating my social media. Various selfies are posted on Instagram, Facebook and Snapchat and witty comments and tips for a better life are posted on Twitter. I reply to my comments and generally weave the impression into my virtual world that I'm living my best life.

As the junior editor of Designer Homes - *on a budget,* I have an impressive social media presence. My words are seized upon and devoured as gospel and along with Sable, we enjoy a mini celebrity style lifestyle. I am always snapping random pictures of ways to get that designer look on a pauper's budget. I've actually become quite good at it and enjoy nothing more than finding a quick fix solution that transforms a room in an afternoon.

Yes, I love my job, but when it comes to my life, the jury's out.

Sometimes I wish I could be more like Sable. Totally committed and unwavering in her pursuit of success. I know how ambitious she is and she won't rest until she's editor-in-chief of Country Living or Elle Decoration. She wants the glass ceiling and knowing her she'll shatter it into a million pieces as she punches her way through. I want it too, or at least that's what I tell myself, but do I – really?

My thoughts are interrupted as a text flashes up on my phone.

Heidi

Happy Birthday, babe. Thirty means flirty, so it's time to reach for your A game. Fancy some drinks after work at the cocacabana rooms?xoxo

I dash off a quick reply.

Lily

Thanks honey, what about 6.30, usual place? xoxo

Heidi

See you then beautiful lady and don't work too hard. xoxo

Smiling, I lean back and think about my friend, Heidi Monroe. Besties since university and poles apart in nearly every way possible. Heidi graduated and ditched her degree almost immediately to open a knitting shop on the outskirts of Tooting. She's a little bohemian and loves the vibrant atmosphere living in a multicultural paradise brings. Her shop is doing well, largely because she's tapped into the yummy mummy brigade who think nouveau knitting is cool. She's great fun though and I couldn't think of anyone I would rather spend my birthday with than her.

Another text pops up from my mum.

Mum

Happy Birthday lovely Lily. I can't believe it's been thirty years since I was in the worst pain I've ever experienced in my life. Who can believe that my body recovered after the copious amounts of blood loss I suffered when I haemorrhaged during the longest labour Nuffield ward had ever seen? Goodness, how time flies when the agonising memory still brings me out in cold sweats in the middle of the night as I deal with nightmares your birth sentenced me to for the rest of my life. Anyway, have a lovely day darling and don't forget to eat a hearty lunch. Soup would be the best option because your metabolic rate slows down when you reach a certain age. Love you - xoxo.

I don't even have time to be annoyed before another message flashes on the screen from my dad.

Dad

Happy Birthday Lily flower. Love you, dad xx.

Short, but infinitely sweeter than my mums. Despite her dubious birthday wishes, I love my mum so much it hurts. She is scatty, forgetful, funny and kind. The only drawback is she has no filter and says things nobody in their right mind would ever voice out loud. Her message was meant to be funny, not unkind and I roll my eyes and giggle at the force of nature who calls herself my mother.

By the time we reach Victoria, I have received eight texts, twenty likes on Facebook, a follow on Instagram and a notification reminding me to book a dentist's appointment. Not bad for an hours commute and as I join the crowd surging toward the underground, I try to raise my spirits and push away the knot in my stomach that sits there as a dull reminder that everything is definitely not ok. Aunt Daisy is dead and life will never be the same again.

Designer homes - *on a budget,* is near Warren Street. Trying not to look at the designer windows of the shops that will be my downfall, I head purposefully toward the place I'll call home until 6pm on the dot. I arrive at 8.30 and leave at 6. Sometimes I have lunch and sometimes I don't; it depends on what's happening. If I'm office bound, I try to get out for some fresh air. If I'm 'out in the field' as they call it at a photo shoot or researching one of our features, I grab something as I go.

Today the only thing of importance is a meeting scheduled with Sable for 9am and my stomach churns as I think about it. She is always 'on it' and if my head is not screwed on 100%, she tears me to shreds inside a minute of being there.

As I make my way to my desk set behind a partition in the open plan office, I can see that Sable is here already. Her office sits at the end of the rather large room behind glass doors and always appears to be a hive of industry. Her assistant Sybil is already in place and I see her tapping away furiously on her computer. Sable herself appears to be doing stretching exercises as her leg is planted firmly on the desk and she is crouched over it limbering up for the gruelling day ahead.

Despite everything, I like my ferocious boss. She is a woman to admire and aspire to be like. She has a sixth sense when it comes to home improvements and her ideas are what made us the number one homes magazine among the budget offerings. Yes, Sable Evans is a power house, much like Aunt Daisy, and I feel a new resolve to be just like them in every way, or die trying.

With my resolution firmly in place, I adjust my attitude and dust off any self-doubts that seep into the cracks of a person who feels like an imposter for most of the day. I can do this; I *am* this. Yes, Lily Rose Adams is the next powerful woman in training and I will not let the side down.

At 8.59 I pass Sybil and smile. "Ok to go in?"

"Oh, hi Lily." She smiles sweetly and I note the frazzled edge that she wears well as she says brightly, "Happy birthday by the way."

"Don't remind me." I grin and she laughs softly, turning her attention back to her screen as she reaches for what is probably her fourth cup of coffee of the morning.

Feeling my heart thumping erratically, I try to act normal as I push my way into certain humiliation.

Sable is facing the window with her back to me talking into her phone and I stand a little awkwardly as I wait for her to finish.

"I'm telling you Roger, it's just not good enough. The builders should have been there two weeks ago and we are already behind schedule. Time costs money, Roger, and you don't need me to remind you that you agreed a fixed price on this job with late penalties. Now, do your job and run your business like a grown up and get those builders doing what you are paying them to do. You have exactly one hour to report back and I had better like what I'm hearing."

She cuts the call and without turning around says sharply, "Bloody project manager, I knew he was weak. Word of advice, Lily, get at least six quotes, four references and sift through the online reviews with a fine toothcomb before appointing any professional person. Smoke and mirrors is what that man excels at and I'm not having it."

She spins around and I feel her sharp stare stripping me bare. I feel uncomfortable as she looks me up and down and assesses everything about me. She cocks her head to one side and I wish I had worn the new Karen Millen dress I bought in the sample sale I went to last week because the River Island one doesn't appear to be passing the test.

It feels a little uncomfortable until she points to the swivel seat in front of her desk. "Sit, darling and listen."

Like an obedient puppy, I do as she says, knowing that if I had a tail, it would be wagging right now because I would do anything to please this woman of greatness who is blessing me with a moment of her time.

She starts to pace around the small glass room and I dig my nails into the palm of my hand as I wait for the words of wisdom to spill from her Elizabeth Arden painted lips.

"Darling, you know I'm an ambitious woman."

I nod, but words are not necessary to answer this particular question. She carries on. "I've been relentless in the pursuit of my dream and even though it hasn't been easy, I have achieved success in a relatively short space of time."

Spinning around, she stares at me long and hard, and I resist the urge to shift on my seat under her intense scrutiny. "You are like me, Lily – driven."

Feeling rather pleased at any comparison to the great one, I smile happily. "Thank you."

She holds up her hand and I fall silent as she carries on. "Yes, ever since you arrived, darling, I have been impressed by what I've seen. You work well, have vision and are not afraid of hard work. Any job I task you with is carried out as I would myself and I have come to rely on you greatly."

Basking in the warm praise I don't often receive, I smile. "Thank you. I have learned from the best."

Nodding, she allows a small smile of agreement to grace her lips and then she perches on the edge of the desk, drumming her fingers on the glass beneath her professionally manicured nails.

"Today is your birthday and as it turns out, is one you will always remember."

Thinking of Aunt Daisy, I have to agree with her and nod sadly. "Sadly yes."

"What do you mean, sadly?"

Her tone is sharp and I say with a sigh. "My Aunt Daisy passed away yesterday. It was unexpected and I'm still trying to come to terms with the fact she's gone."

Shaking her head, Sable says quickly, "That's very unfortunate. You have my condolences."

Unfortunate is a strange choice of word but I brush it off and say softly, "Thank you."

"Anyway." She carries on and I know the subject is now closed. Business does and always will come first with Sable, so I resign myself to hearing my orders for the day.

"Times are changing, Lily. The high street is in decline and magazines are being cast aside for the virtual world. Sustainability is the new buzz word and paying cash for a fallen tree made into pretty pictures is no longer considered the right thing to do. Now our readers devour our wisdom on their phones, computers and tablets. We are evolving and in an increasingly rapidly changing landscape. We at Designer Homes - *on a budget,* embrace change. We lap up this new world as if we are starving and will never get enough. We are evolving, Lily, which is why the future is so exciting."

I stare at Sable in astonishment as she stands looking so animated, I almost want to take a photo to pin on my inspiration mood board on Pinterest. Wow, Sable is possessed by the spirit of evolution and I hold my breath waiting for the pearls of wisdom to spill into my eager ears.

"I'm leaving, Lily, stepping down and moving on. Packing my bags and walking away."

As she looks at me with a triumphant smile, I am speechless.

♥3

What?!

For a moment, I struggle to understand what she's just said. Finally, my voice shakes as I say, "Leaving... but you can't."

She laughs and the look on her face tells me that wherever she's going is epic because I have never seen her looking so excited.

"I know you're surprised, darling, but I've been thinking of it for some time. Arthur and I decided that we need to embrace a new life and use our skills to benefit our future."

Thinking about Sable's new husband, I wonder how much more enrichment their life needs. They have a comfortable life already because he's an architect and not short of money and they met through a feature she ran on one of his projects.

She carries on. "Yes, we have decided to up sticks and move away to a brave new world."

"What - the country?" I stare at her in horror as I imagine Sable in a pair of Barbour wellies with a golden retriever by her tweed-covered side.

"No darling, not the country, *a* country. France to be exact."

"France! But why?"

I am struggling to get my head around this information. Sable has London running through her veins. She belongs here in the sophisticated world she rules. Not France.

Gathering my wits together, I say "Paris, are you setting up a Paris office?"

To me this makes more sense and I feel myself relaxing. Yes, Paris, of course, chic and on trend. Definitely the place I imagine Sable moving to.

She laughs shrilly, "Not Paris, darling, Provence. Arthur and I have bought a crumbing Château set in fifty acres. We intend on renovating it and converting it to a place of business. You know the sort of thing, weddings, corporate events and an exclusive hotel. There will be gîtes and shooting and of course, there's the vineyard to keep us going."

I feel weak as I try to absorb the details of Sable's brave new world.

She says excitedly. "We've been thinking of it for some time. It's perfect in every way. Arthur will design the new venture and I will project manage it. I will use my skills to film a daily vlog on our experience and use my social skills to drum up interest and hopefully land a television series. Yes, we are going big on this, Lily, as I'm sure you would expect."

She moves across and takes her seat behind her desk, leaning forward and saying earnestly, "Which brings me to you."

"Me?"

My mind is spinning as I try to understand what she just said as she says loudly, "I want you to take my place, Lily. Step up as editor-in-chief of Designer Homes - *on a budget*."

There is a roaring sound in my head as I struggle to let her words sink in. Me - editor-in-chief! I can't believe it. She laughs at my shocked expression. "Push away those doubts darling, you could do this standing on your head. It's what you've been trained to do, and I have the full support of the suits upstairs. They agree you are the perfect replacement and we are to go straight from here to meet them for a glass of champagne and to sign your new contract."

My head spins and I can't form words. This is huge. Too much to take in and I can't breathe. Me – editor-in-chief – I made it.

Sable laughs and carries on, glossing over any shock her words have delivered. "It all works out rather well. We will move into one of the gîtes while the Château is refurbished. Arthur will work from France and it's just a quick train journey to bring him to London when required."

Work from France! I thought working from home was a luxury but working from France, ooh la la.

As her words seep into my rational thought, I feel the excitement growing and forcing out any doubts I have. I can do this - I can. She's right, I will be the best editor-in-chief this magazine has ever had, and if she could see me now, Aunt Daisy would be impressed. I'm just like her – a successful woman at the top of my game.

I want to punch the air and scream the place down. I want to run around the office jumping from desk to desk. I want to swivel around the office in my chair, waving my hands like a madwoman, and I want to announce it on social media with a picture of me looking so smug it will become my new profile picture. I can update my status as editor-in-chief and update my LinkedIn profile and prove that I was always one of them – the successful women who I followed religiously.

Maybe I'll set up a club for successful women only, and we will share tips and news to help and encourage each other. I will attend forums and power dress. I will start drinking green tea and wearing my hair in chignons. I may even buy some glasses to make me look the part and I will glide rather than walk as only powerful woman do.

I have almost forgotten that Sable is in the room as I start redesigning her office. It will be streamlined and chic. I will have an open-door policy and will be the most loved boss in history. My staff will be my new family and cheer me as I deliver yet another record-breaking issue. This is it – I've arrived and I never knew it. Thirty is amazing because within one day of turning the big three o, I have achieved my life's ambition.

Sable interrupts me planning my celebratory party and says quickly, "Right, first we'll head upstairs to see Mr Mitchell and Mr Stevens. Then we will toast your new role with champagne and take some photographs for the next edition. After that we will work out a press release and inform the staff."

My head is spinning as I struggle to keep up and then she says softly, "I know this is a lot to take in, darling. Once this is all over maybe you should start thinking of what needs doing before the big day."

"What do you mean?" I look at her in confusion and she sighs. "This job will become your life. Every hour of your day will be taken up with it. It offers huge rewards but desires a huge sacrifice on your part. No more free time because every minute of your day will be spent thinking of what needs to be done. My advice to you is to take all your holidays within three months because that's my notice period. Do all the things you always wanted to, take a holiday, learn a new skill, I don't know, live a lifetime in a few short weeks because then the real work starts."

"But I don't need…" She holds up her hand and looks quite ferocious. "I know what you're about to say but take it from one who knows. You think this is everything and it is. But use this time wisely and make some time for yourself before it's taken away from you. You will understand what I mean when the hard work begins, so trust me now."

I nod, not really believing her, and she says softly. "Congratulations, darling. You deserve every minute of your success."

Just for a moment, we stare at each other. The mentor and the protegee shifting roles. The tears spring to my eyes as I realise what this means.

She's leaving. She's actually leaving and I will no longer have anyone to hide behind. No more sounding board who tells me my ideas won't work and the reasons why. No one to offer me encouragement and call me out on any bad decisions. No one to impress, hoping to draw an appreciative remark or smile from the lips of a goddess.

My voice breaks slightly as I say, "I'll miss you, Sable."

To my surprise, I see a tear in her eye as she nods. "I know."

Then she stands and holds out her hand, and as I grasp it, she shakes it firmly. "Be the best, Lily, you owe it to yourself. Be everything you ever wanted to be and do it well. You are a strong woman and deserve every minute of your success. Take Designer Homes - *on a budget* and make it shine. You've got this, darling. I believe in you."

Her words mean everything to me as does she and as we walk upstairs to the management suite, I make a silent promise to not let her down.

♥ 4

"Aargh, I can't breathe, I can't speak, I can't believe it."

Laughing, I grin at Heidi and take a moment to enjoy her reaction. Today is the start of my new life in charge and competent, and it feels good to have a friend to share it with.

Then I laugh for another reason as I look at the sight before me. To say that Heidi loves her job is an understatement. Today she is wearing a hand knitted stripy bobble hat and matching scarf. Bright pink leggings are tucked inside white furry ski boots, and her huge padded jacket is as white as the snow. Her eyes shine behind her tortoiseshell glasses and her bright pink lips are turned in a smile as she celebrates my news. Heidi was always eccentric which developed more as she grew older. Not caring what the world thinks, she goes about life with a don't care attitude and positivity. Her shop is doing well and time is as precious to her as it is to me, which is why I relish our little meetings because increasingly she is the only friend I have.

Shaking her head, her smile is wide and infectious.

"Congratulations, Lily. You completely deserve this. I can't believe how much happiness I will get when I name drop about my bestie who runs Designer Homes - *on a budget*. Way to go, I'm so proud of you."

My smug look is firmly now a feature on my face as I bask in the glory of my appointment. Yes, life is good, for some of us anyway and as I think about Aunt Daisy, my face must fall a little because Heidi says with some concern, "What's the matter, aren't you happy?"

"Of course, I am but the timing's a little off."

"Why?"

"Because of Aunt Daisy. I wish she could have been here and heard my news. She would have been so proud; I suppose I feel a little short-changed because she will never know how far I've come."

Reaching across the table, Heidi grips my hand tightly. "If you believe, as I certainly do, in the afterlife, you will know she is here with you now."

Feeling slightly alarmed, I look around me and whisper, "Do you think?"

"Absolutely and if I know how these things work, she probably had a hand in it herself - you know, a parting gift to keep the family flag flying. Handing over the responsibility to immortalise the women in your family to greatness. Yes, Aunt Daisy knows, Lily and will be watching every step you take."

Pulling away, she holds up the menu and squints. "I think I'll go for the vegetarian option."

"Since when?"

She grins. "I'm not a vege yet, but I'm thinking about it. You know, all this talk about Veganuary, it's got me thinking."

"But you don't like vegetables, what will you eat?"

Shrugging, Heidi leans back and grins. "I like potatoes."

"You can't live on potatoes."

"Then I will partake of that meat substitute they are raving about. Yes, it's worth a shot at least."

The waiter heads over and smiles. "Are you ready to order?"

Nodding, and with a determined glint in her eye, Heidi says loudly, "I would like the meat-free lasagne please."

I stifle a giggle as he says "Vegetable lasagne then. And for you…?"

He turns to me and I grin. "Sirloin steak please with fries and peppercorn sauce. Does that come with vegetables?"

He nods. "Au gratin."

"Perfect, oh and a large glass of red wine please and the same for my friend, we're celebrating."

He looks interested. "Sounds good, is it your birthday?"

"Yes, but don't even ask my age. Oh, and I've got a promotion, so it's doubly good."

Looking impressed, the waiter nods. "Then congratulations and enjoy your meal."

As he heads off, Heidi sighs. "I wish men would look at me the way they do you."

"Like what?" I'm surprised because in my mind he looked at me no differently than anyone else.

"Like he wanted you."

I almost spit out my water. "Wanted me, you're deluded."

"No, I'm not." She shakes her head and folds her arms, and I know that look – the one that means business. "Men look at you as if they want to own you. There's a hunger in their eyes that has nothing to do with the food you order. They are attracted to you and don't know how to deal with it. You know, if only one man looked at me in that way, I would unravel like a ball of wool. It's just not fair, some women have it all."

"Says the girl who has a new date every week."

She grins and shakes her head. "That's true, but none of them ever throw me *that* look. It's why there's a different one every week because I'm still looking."

"What about the guy who played tennis?"

"What, the pro at the club in town?"

"Yes, if I remember rightly, he was the one. You know, Tom, Tom, he's the one."

Heidi grins. "He was the one until I discovered I was one of two, or was it three? You see my darling Lily; men are not to be trusted. They spin a tale they think you want to hear and reel you in. Then, when they've had their wicked way with you, they move onto the next one. No ties, no obligations, no worries. You, on the other hand, you could have it all if you wanted it but you don't even realise the power you have. You are so weighed down with your issues you can't see the wood for the trees."

The waiter returns with our drinks and I almost can't make eye contact with him. When I do, I feel a little faint as he stares at me with a kind of hunger in his eyes and for a little longer than necessary. Heidi is actually gloating as the smirk on her face reveals her point and I am so flustered I revert to the idiot inside me and say quickly, "Thank you," and grasp the glass so quickly the contents splash all over the tablecloth and the stem of the glass breaks in my hand. The glass drops to the table and I'm so surprised I rock back on my seat and it gives out beneath me and ricochets across the room, leaving me lying on my back staring up into the horrified eyes of the waiter, while Heidi bursts out laughing.

Just for a moment, there is silence all around and then he appears to shake himself and spring to attention, offering me his hand to pull me to my feet. As I take hold, his hand closes around mine and I swear he rubs my thumb with his and gives it an extra squeeze. As soon as I'm on my feet, I snatch my hand away and glare at Heidi, who is filming the whole thing on her phone. "Stop that Heidi, I don't want to see one frame of that on Facebook."

I hear the gentle sound of laughter like a whisper in the breeze all around me and the waiter says with concern, "Are you ok? Would you like me to call an ambulance?"

Feeling my cheeks flame, I say weakly, "No thanks, I'm fine. Just the chair please, oh and maybe a screen, you know, the sort that will hide me away from the rest of civilisation while I work out how I got to be so clumsy."

His lips twitch as he tries to disguise the laughter, and I shake my head. "I'm sorry about the wine glass, please add it to my bill."

I watch as his eyes soften and he says, "I won't hear of it. In fact, I will refresh your drink on the house, call it a birthday present from me to you."

Once again, I feel uncomfortable as he throws me *that* look and I say quickly, "You are very kind. Anyway, the chair would be good when you're ready."

As he turns away, I say loudly, "Thank goodness that didn't happen when I was out with um… Kevin, Heidi. I would never live it down."

She shakes her head as I waffle on about the imaginary Kevin. "Yes, it's our anniversary you know and I think he's going to propose. Could you imagine if we lost the ring because of my clumsiness?"

Heidi shakes her head as the waiter retrieves my chair, looking a little disheartened. He makes sure I'm sitting and then heads off looking dejected and Heidi says crossly, "Why did you do that, he was nice?"

"Do what?"

"Do everything you could to put him off with imaginary Kevin. You know, Lily, one day you will actually have to leave your imaginary boyfriend in the past and grab yourself a real one. It won't be

35

difficult, as I said, you appear to be some kind of man magnet."

Gloomily, I reach for the water and as I take a sip of the cool liquid, it brings me to my senses. I'm such an idiot. I don't know what I'm so scared of, really. Maybe it's because my last boyfriend turned out to be married with children. Maybe it's because the one before him had a possessive streak and used to turn up at the office and stand across the road until I came out, then insisted on walking me to the station even though he was going in the opposite direction. I've never been lucky in love, which is why I'm happy to concentrate on my career, it's for the best, for me, anyway.

More red wine arrives, and this time the waiter is silent. Once he's gone, Heidi draws out a brightly wrapped package and thrusts it towards me. "Happy birthday, I've got you a present."

I stare at her in surprise and feel a lump in my throat. "A present – for me. That's so kind of you."

Taking the small package in my hand, I feel like a kid again as she says softly, "What else did you get?"

"Nothing."

"What do you mean, nothing? Surely your mum and dad bought you something, what about your grandparents, they always buy you things?"

As I start to unwrap the parcel, I shrug with indifference. "Mum and dad deposited fifty pounds into my account and sent a text tag. Nan and Grandpa Forest sent me a gift voucher for Costa and

Nan and Granddad Adams sent me ten pounds in a card. Mark always forgets and Aunt Daisy… well…"

I blink away the tears and Heidi looks concerned. "So, this is the first actual gift you're unwrapping? I feel a little pressure now."

"Why?"

"Because it's rubbish."

"Thanks, you bought me rubbish."

I grin and she shakes her head. "No, it's just something I made. It's not worth anything, and I feel bad that it's the only thing you'll get. You know, that's another reason to look for a man. They give good presents if you throw enough hints in their general direction."

As I unwrap the gift, it could be a chocolate bar for all I care. The fact she took time to actually make me something is worth far more than any present costing actual money.

Inside the packaging is a cardboard box with Pritt Stick written on the side, and she smiles guiltily. "I begged that from the stationery shop next door. They are very obliging when it comes to recycling their waste. Probably because it costs a small fortune to get it collected."

Looking at the small box, I don't think it would save them much, but as I pull the contents out, I smile happily as Heidi says somewhat apologetically. "I hope you don't mind but I made you happy socks."

"Happy socks? Why are they happy?"

37

"Because they're bright and loud and guaranteed to bring a smile to the face of anyone who sees you wearing them."

As I pull out the odd, multi-striped, rather long socks, I can see that any sane person would laugh if they saw someone actually wearing these. However, in my eyes, they couldn't be more perfect.

Feeling quite emotional, I say with tears in my eyes, "Thank you, they're astonishing."

Heidi laughs. "You can say that again. I was experimenting with designs and decided they were a little too 'out there' for normal consumption. So, who better than my bestie to wear them with pride? You will wear them – won't you?"

She looks a little anxious and I smile. "Maybe not in public but I will love wearing them around my flat. Is that ok, you won't be offended if I don't wear them to work or anything?"

Laughing, she shakes her head. "As if. No, I'm extremely aware of my design limitations. Anyway, what's next then in this amazing life you've got stretching before you?"

"I suppose I'll be training with Sable for the majority of the next three months and we have Aunt Daisy's funeral, of course. After that, I suppose it's all systems go."

Raising her glass to mine, she says with determination. "Happy birthday, Lily Rose Adams. May the year ahead deliver your dreams."

As we clink glasses, I can't help feeling that it already has.

♥ 5

Aunt Daisy's house is as impressive as the lady herself. As we park the car outside, there's a brief moment of silence as we look at the modern structure of a home with not a blade of grass out of place. Dad sighs and says somewhat wistfully, "Such a waste."

"What, the house or her life?"

Mum is straight to the point as always and dad just shakes his head. "Both I suppose. I mean, Daisy worked so hard to get this and put everything into it. She had no life outside of her business and what was the point of it all in the end?"

Mum nods and reaching out, rubs his arm in sympathy. "I suppose it made her happy. She thrived on this life she led. It was all she ever wanted and she got there by hard work and determination."

"Yes, but what did it really get her in the end? Dying alone with nobody to carry on her legacy. She never had children and after the dust settles, she will just be that woman who did well for herself and then died."

"Honestly David, what a way to speak of your sister. She will be remembered by all of *us,* for starters. Then there are her friends and business associates. I'm pretty sure she will go down in history among the interior design circles and, after all, it was what she wanted. All of this."

Mum waves her hand around and dad shrugs. "Maybe you're right but I'd trade all of this for the life I have with you and the kids."

For a moment mum appears lost for words, and as they look at each other, I see the love of a shared life pass between them. Yes, in many ways they are richer than Aunt Daisy because they have each other and two children who will always be there for them. That is, when Mark comes back from his gap year in Australia, but I'm always here.

As we head towards the house, I wonder if Aunt Daisy ever wanted to meet anyone and have children. She always said she didn't and I can see her now, rolling her eyes and laughing, saying, "Why would I want all that baggage weighing me down, when all I want to do is fly and see how high I can go?"

Yes, Aunt Daisy wanted to scale the heights of success, not roll around on the ground with the rest of us as we try to dig ourselves out of the rut that normal people always appear to fall into despite their best efforts.

As dad inserts the spare key into the lock, we wait for him to do the mad dash to the security control panel before the alarm goes off. As soon as the coast is clear, we make our way inside and I look around feeling an overwhelming sadness that I will never see her again.

Mum shakes her head and says sadly, "This house never seemed lived in to me."

Dad grins. "If you mean because there are no shoes cluttering up the hallway and the floors are clean and swept, then I'm all for 'not' lived in. You know, maybe we could learn a trick or two from Daisy and go minimalist.

"Minimalist, David! Are you joking with me? Who drops his shoes on the floor as soon as he steps foot inside the door? Who chucks his coat over the bannisters and his briefcase on the mat? Who, may I ask, leaves the toilet seat up and the towel scrunched on the side and who apparently hasn't yet grasped the concept of actually closing cupboards and drawers when he opens them? Oh, and who…"

"Enough, I get the picture."

Dad grins and mum shakes her head, looking slightly annoyed. "It was all well and good for Daisy, she only had to deal with her own mess. Not pick up after an ungrateful bunch of humans who think the fairies do it. I'm thinking Daisy had the right idea and made the right choice in life because I'm guessing she never had to scrub the toothpaste off the sink and rearrange the cushions every time somebody…" She frowns at my father. "Leaves them all over the place. You know, David, you have a very messy sitting habit, has anyone ever told you that?"

"Messy sitting habit, what's that when it's at home?"

"I just told you. Your bottom appears to churn up every throw, cushion and seat pad on the settee that you never feel the need to straighten. If I had one pound for…"

I tune out and wander off, leaving them to their daily argument of what annoys them most about each other. It's the usual conversation, and as I pass through the polished rooms of perfection, I feel as if Aunt Daisy had it all worked out.

Surely everyone wants what she had? The trappings of success to greet you when you come home at night, reminding you that it was all worth it. The air smells clean and fragrant and almost pure, and if the house seems a little soulless, then it's because that's what made Aunt Daisy happy. Yes, she would have a very clear mind living here where she could relax in comfort after a hard day making even more money and not have anyone moaning to disrupt her inner calm.

Mum comes up behind me and says softly, "Shall we all take a room each?"

Nodding, I think about the reason we're here at all. Dad decided that we should remove any items of value or personal interest while the house is standing empty. Until the Will is read, we don't know who benefits from Aunt Daisy's passing and he is concerned thieves may be aware she has died and break in one night. I agreed to help, but now I'm here, I wish I hadn't. It doesn't feel right to be looking through her private possessions, when she isn't even buried yet.

Mum puts her arm around me. "It's what she would have wanted, love. Don't feel bad. Surely she would want us to keep her valuables safe for whoever she left them to. Now, I'll take the kitchen, dad's doing the study and you can start upstairs if you like? Maybe her bedroom is the best place to begin."

As she walks away, I wish I had the kitchen. It wouldn't feel as personal as delving through her drawers and rifling through her clothes. Some may still have the lingering trace of Chanel number 5 on them, which I will always associate with her. She adored it and sprayed it liberally whenever she could.

Then, I realise the real reason I'm so reluctant is because she died in her bedroom. Just the thought of her lying in bed alone and hopefully asleep when it happened, gives me the shivers. What if her spirit still lingers between Heaven and Earth? What if she's watching me now and is angry that we're invading her personal space like this?

It's almost too much to bear, and I can feel a panic attack coming on and almost give up before I even start. However, there's also the part of me that relishes some form of contact with the woman I admired so much. Just the smell of her perfume, or seeing a familiar outfit, will bring her back to me. I wasn't prepared to never see her again when she left after lunch two Sundays ago. Maybe I would have said things that mattered, instead of whining on about being single at thirty. Aunt Daisy never whined. She never complained and approached life with a can-do attitude. She was amazing in every way, and I can't believe I'll never see her again.

As I venture into her freakishly large bedroom, the scent hits me as I knew it would. Tears spring to my eyes and as I brush them away, I can almost hear her saying in the gentle tone she always used around me, "No need to cry, honey, what's done is done. Don't dwell on things you can't change and concentrate instead on the ones you can."

Ok, she was talking at the time about that creep I was dating who turned out to be married with kids, but the principle is the same.

Moving across to her dressing table, I decide to start there because I just can't face the prospect of feeling the fabric of her clothes. Taking each of the drawers in turn, I empty the contents and go through them, checking for items of jewellery or anything of value. The rest I place back where it was because whoever gets this place can deal with it when it happens.

I almost feel like one of the thieves they fear as I place items of jewellery into the soft bag I found inside one of the drawers. It appears that Aunt Daisy had a keen eye because the items she bought are exquisite. Beautiful rings, bracelets and necklaces glitter in their velvet-lined drawers. Designer watches nestle proudly inside a watch winder as they wait to be selected to match a certain outfit. There is none of the rubbish, bits of fluff, or sweet wrappers that sit inside my drawers at home.

These are kept immaculate and I feel ashamed at my own dirty ways.

It doesn't take long before I move to the walk-in wardrobe and gasp with pleasure at the array of clothing hanging in colour matched blocks, looking as if they have never been worn. A soft pile cream carpet is pure heaven beneath my feet, and the drawers of cashmere jumpers and silky underwear bring out the girlie girl inside me. Shelves upon shelves of amazing shoes and handbags tempt me, and glittering evening gowns twinkle from the furthest corners as the spotlights pick out the sparkle woven into the fabric.

This is every woman's dream and suddenly I understand Aunt Daisy and her choices in life because who wouldn't want this life of luxury?

Leaving most things untouched, I concentrate on the highest shelves where there are big white boxes tied with satin ribbon. Inside are various personal items, and as I take the first one down, I sit on her bed and start sifting through. I'm amazed to see one is full of photographs and spend a large amount of time looking through them, enjoying seeing Aunt Daisy's life in glorious colour before my eyes. She has been everywhere it seems and the snapshot of a well-travelled life, makes me determined to do the same. Exotic locations and beautiful sandy beaches show Aunt Daisy laughing at the camera, usually with a brightly coloured cocktail in her hand. It strikes me that there is never anyone else in the picture. Just her and I wonder about the people who took them. Were they strangers she asked to immortalise the moment for her, or did she travel with a willing companion we never got to meet?

I am so engrossed in my task, I don't realise how long we've been here until my mother shouts from the doorway, "Do you fancy a cuppa, darling? Dad thinks his throat's been cut. I think there's some milk, but I can't be sure if it's turned or not. Come down if you fancy it but be warned, you may have to take it black."

Shaking myself, I look around the room with a new resolve. Yes, I want this. I want what she had – all of it. This has confirmed that I was always meant to live this life. I'm glad I came because it's given me the reassurance I need.

As I finish up, I glance around and think I've covered most of it. Maybe I should start on the guest room next. Turning to place the boxes back on the shelves, I notice a small notebook laying on the highest shelf preventing me from sliding the box back. Grabbing the nearby chair, I jump on it to retrieve the notebook and as I feel the soft leather in my hands, my curiosity wins over any cup of tea. Once again, I sit on the bed and open the book, loving the rich coloured cream paper with gold edging. I've always loved a good notebook and this is the stuff of dreams.

I hear my mum calling and hastily place the book in my bag and head off to see what they're up to downstairs.

♥6

Just as I reach the last step, the doorbell rings and mum rushes out of the kitchen looking resigned. "That'll be nanny and granddad. They said they'd stop by and help." She rolls her eyes. "Hinder more like. You know, we'll get on far better if we were just left alone, this is all I need."

She mutters under her breath as she answers the door and as I see my grandparents standing there, it brings a lump to my throat because I have never seen them looking so frail. The grief is etched in every line and wrinkle on their faces and they appear to have aged ten years since I last saw them.

Nan's eyes fill with tears as she steps into my mum's arms and breaks down, sobbing uncontrollably. I can't help but join in because this scene is devastating. Dad ventures out of the study and shouts loudly, "Now, now, Daisy wouldn't want this. Come on, let's leave those tears outside and remember happier times."

Granddad wipes a tear away and appears to steel himself as he straightens his back and places a comforting hand on his wife's back. As she pulls away, her eyes find mine and her lip trembles as she staggers towards me, her arms outstretched. "Lily, darling, such terrible news."

My heart shatters as she falls into my arms and as I hug her hard, I feel her body wracked with grief. She mumbles tearfully, "It isn't right, it should be me, not her, not my beautiful baby girl."

I'm not sure what to say because there are no words. No mother should ever survive her daughter and I cannot imagine how she must be feeling. Mum pulls her away and says gently, "Come on, Sandra, Daisy wouldn't want you to work yourself up into a state. She's at peace now and probably didn't even know anything about it. It's how I want to go, tucked up in bed and none the wiser. Now, I've made a nice pot of tea and found some of those posh biscuits from Fortnum's she loved. Let's go and remember Daisy how she would want us to."

She helps nan away and pulls her into the kitchen and the rest of us follow, feeling as low as a person can get. Grief is hard to deal with and especially only days after the person who was larger than life was taken. It's all a bit surreal and as mum busies herself making the tea, we all crowd around the large island unit that dominates the designer kitchen and stare at each other with glum expressions.

Dad pipes up, "I found lots of stuff in the study that I'm taking to keep safe. You know, important documents and some credit cards and money. Her handbag was in there, so we should take that as well and make a list of all the companies she has cards with and inform them."

"You'll need the death certificate, I think." Nan interrupts and dad says kindly, "Do you want me to arrange everything?"

Nan nods and looks across at grandad, who smiles gently. "Maybe that would be for the best, son. I'm not sure we're firing on all cylinders most of time, let alone now. Just do our Daisy proud with whatever you choose and we will help out where we can."

Mum passes the drinks across and turns to me. "Did you find anything, Lily?"

"I've found her jewellery and watches, maybe nan should have them and keep them safe."

I push the bag across the counter and nan's eyes fill with tears as she pulls out a beautiful bracelet. "She always loved a bit of sparkle did Daisy. She was our little star, wasn't she Bert?"

He nods as nan pulls out the contents of the bag and appears to just want to feel the items her daughter treasured so highly. Remembering the notebook, I pull it out and say softly, "I also found this. Maybe you should have this as well."

Nan looks astonished and laughing, turns to granddad. "Look Bert, do you remember this? I can't believe she kept it after all these years."

He nods. "Well I'll be... fancy seeing this again."

"What is it?" Mum looks as interested as I am and we inadvertently lean forward so as not to miss a thing. "It's that old notebook she used to write in when she was a teenager. She was forever scribbling something in it, she was such a funny little girl."

She opens it and we can see Aunt Daisy's neat writing covering the cream pages and nan laughs. "She was always a planner, you know. Used to make lists and everything and took great delight in crossing them off as she achieved them. Look at this, she's even put the date." Peering at it closely, she shakes her head. "She must have been fifteen when she wrote this, look Bert, she's called it her life goals."

She laughs and I can see that she's remembering back to when Daisy was fifteen as she reads them out loud.

1 - Be successful.

2 - Be successful.

3 - Be successful.

Mum interrupts. "I think she could safely cross the first three off her list."

We all laugh and nan smiles. "She was always a determined young lady. I think she inherited that from me."

Grandad rolls his eyes behind her back and I stifle a grin. To my knowledge, nan never worked and stayed home to bring up the family. Grandad, however, was a powerhouse in his youth and very successful. He started several companies and built a mini empire. He was driven, unrelenting and a force to be reckoned with, and if Daisy took after anyone, it was him.

Nan carries on with the list.

"4 - Be happy.

5 - Be healthy.

6 - Be organised."

Once again, they laugh and mum says, "I've never met anyone as organised as she was. She's definitely rocking that list."

"7 - Find my soulmate."

The room falls silent as we discover the first thing she failed at. Unlucky number seven.

Dad says with curiosity, "Did she ever find him - her soulmate that is? I don't think I ever met him if she did."

Nan shakes her head sadly. "There were a few gentlemen friends but no one special. She always told me she never had time for a personal life and you should have heard the arguments we had over it, honestly, they could hear us shouting in the next street."

Thinking of the photographs upstairs, I wonder again who took them and say with interest, "Did she ever go on holiday with anyone? I found some old photos upstairs of Aunt Daisy in all sorts of places. She was always smiling into the camera, so I wondered if she travelled with the person who took them?"

Laughing, nan shakes her head. "I'm sure there were many men, darling. Daisy wasn't afraid of meeting them; it was keeping them that was the problem. You see, she was an attractive woman with prospects. The men would flock to her feet in their droves and I know she wasn't averse to playing with the toys on offer."

Mum looks shocked and I giggle. Goodness, Aunt Daisy was wild. Who would have thought?

Nan says thoughtfully. "There was this one man, I think she was in her mid-twenties, maybe twenty-six, I can't remember. Anyway, she seemed smitten with him and for a moment there, I thought we'd have to raid the bank to pay for the wedding we always thought we'd fund one day."

Now I'm interested. "What happened?"

She shrugs. "I'm not sure. I know she was devastated, whatever it was. I did ask, but she had this way about her that kept personal things inside behind steel shutters and she would never say. However, I do know it knocked her back for a bit. I could tell she wasn't herself and all she would say is, if you don't have your health you have nothing."

I'm sure the same thought occurs to us all, as we realise the truth to her words. Yes, she may have had everything, but her health let her down in the end and it was all for nothing at the end of the day.

Dad pipes up, "She once told me about a Simon Grainger."

Grandad nods. "That's the one. I remember the name because Grainger was the name of the captain of the golf club at the time. I think it must have been his son because Daisy told me his dad played golf."

Nan nods. "Yes, that's right. I think it was serious for a while, but then one day when I asked her how things were going, she shot me down and told me to butt out of her life and there was never any mention of him again. I thought she'd found out he was married like the rest of them and never thought anything of it."

Thinking back on my own encounter with a married man, I can sympathise with Aunt Daisy. Goodness, we are more alike than I thought.

Nan nods sadly. "Yes, I remember now. Good-looking young man; I had high hopes for him. Never mind, not everything works out in life."

"I think he died from blood poisoning."

We all look at grandad and he nods. "Yes, the deputy captain told me the captain's son had cut his foot on a rusty nail in the garden and died of blood poisoning. It was quite unexpected really."

Dad raises his eyes and says loudly, "What else is on the list?"

Squinting, nan carries on. "8 - Have children."

She wipes another tear away and mum takes the book from her hand, smiling gently. "Here, let me. 9 - Travel the world.

10 - Dance under the stars with the man you've just kissed.

11 - Sing in the rain.

12 - Watch a movie with a stranger.

13 - Take dance lessons.

14 - Sing in a crowd.

15 - Camp out under the stars.

16 - Help someone who needs it.

17 - Do something spontaneous.

18 - Go for a walk by the sea and gather shells.

19 - Compliment yourself every day in the mirror.

20 - Take a hot-air balloon flight.

21 – Exercise.

22 - Paint a naked man."

Nan laughs out loud. "Dirty cow."

We all laugh and mum says rather red-faced, "If you think that one was bad you should hear number 23."

We look at her expectantly and she giggles, "Have sex with a stranger on the beach."

Nan whips the book from her hand and shakes her head. "Lucky cow, that one's ticked."

As she snatches the book, a loose piece of paper falls out and we look at it in surprise. Reaching out, I unfold it and say with interest, "She wrote herself a letter."

"Read it." Nan's voice sounds strangled and I see the tears gathering once again, and as grandad puts his arm around her, I begin to read.

"Dear Daisy.

It's been thirty years since you wrote the goals you vowed to live your life by. Looking back on them it appears you managed a few, but for some reason most of them remain to be done. On reflection, I should have placed a different one at the top of the list because now I know that was the one every woman should value above all others.

Happiness. If you have happiness, the rest cease to matter.

Congratulations on achieving success three times over. Surely you have everything you ever wanted, but it brings with it a huge dose of loneliness.

I have learned that having material possessions is nothing if you have no one to share it with. When love was so cruelly snatched away from me, I shut myself off from finding it again with someone else. I made myself richer, more successful and emotionless. The purpose of this letter is to remind myself that life is not to be mapped out from the beginning, but a journey of discovery and self-development. The main thing now is to take stock of the situation and make changes before it's too late because I don't want to die alone."

Mum's voice shakes as we stand silently, listening to the saddest letter I have ever heard in my life. The tears fall from every pair of eyes in the room as she continues.

"I now have a different set of priorities that I fear I may have left too late. Now is the time to search for love and make a future with the man I love. It may be too late to start a family, but we could adopt, maybe. I want the dream and that is love. I want to tick every last item off my list because I wrote them for a reason. I don't want to grow old and have regrets of a wasted life in the pursuit of money above everything. I want to know

that I gave it my best shot and took the life I was blessed with and made it count for something.

Daisy, this is the first letter you have written to yourself and I hope it won't be the last. Maybe the next one will be to my child, or my husband. Maybe the next one will be to my grandchildren, and maybe the next one will be to congratulate myself on learning what matters in life and fulfilling everything I set out to do.

So, stop, take stock of your life and chart a different heading because the world is a better place to travel beside someone you love and loves you back just as much.

Yours, hopefully
Daisy Adams."

Mum wipes a tear away and says with a break in her voice. "She's added a PS. *You have three years to make this happen Daisy, don't let me down.*"

♥ 7

When I wake the next morning, the first thing I see is Aunt Daisy's notebook. Reaching out, I take the book and sit back against the pillows and carry on where I left off late last night. After we heard the letter, there was much discussion and unanimously everyone thought I should be the notebook's beneficiary and that was fine by me.

Last night I devoured every word of it.

The list went on for another twenty points and painted a picture of a woman who wanted to live her life to the full and beyond. There were even several Venn diagrams plotting her way to success with happiness at the centre of every one of them. Little cut outs of inspirational quotes were stuck in with Sellotape, along with lists of places to visit enabling her to fulfil a certain item on the list.

Even now my head is spinning as I contemplate the enormity of the task in hand because last night, I made my own vow to myself. I will not be Aunt Daisy and have regrets. I'll do as many things on this list as possible and do them in three months because after that, my brave new world will be upon me and I'll have no time to do any of it, if Sable is right about the workload heading my way.

This time as I take the train to work, it's a different journey I take. There is no social media to occupy my time. Instead, I read the notebook and engulf myself in resolve. I *will* do this and I *can* do this. Yes, I will have lived a lifetime of memories before I take on my ultimate dream and I'll have no regrets.

Sable, as usual, is in her office and as I knock tentatively on the door, she looks up and smiles. "Morning, Lily. Are you ready and eager to get started on the rest of your life?"

Edging inside, I say nervously, "You could say that."

She raises her eyes and I say quickly, "If it's ok with you, I would like to use some of the holiday I have stacked up."

Looking thoughtful, she nods. "Good idea. What do you need, one week… two weeks?"

"Um… I think I have four weeks owed. Is it ok if I take it all at once?"

She looks a little put out and I say quickly, "It's just that with Aunt Daisy passing, it's made me look at things a little differently. There are many things I want to do before my time is taken up with the magazine. If I do them now, it will enable me to fully focus on my career and who knows, I may learn a thing or two in the process?"

Looking interested, Sable points to the seat in front of her desk. "Tell me, what are your plans?"

Swallowing hard, I perch nervously on the edge of the seat. "Well, I would like to go on holiday and maybe take a class in something, um… art perhaps?"

"Hmm, not a bad idea. Ok, darling, four weeks it is and not a day more. It will give me time to train your replacement as deputy editor and then, when you return, I can give you my full attention."

"My replacement?"

I feel a little put out, I mean, surely, I should appoint my deputy and Sable narrows her eyes. "Yes, I need to appoint someone who I know will be up to the job. You won't know what's needed yet because you haven't walked in my shoes. I have and they are painful, so now is the time to set the wheels in motion for the continued success of this company. Trust me, darling, I always know best."

She drums her fingers on the desk and smiles. "You see, women like me leave no stone left unturned. Take the Château, for example. The builders are now working like a well-oiled machine, and every eventuality has been entered on a spreadsheet and planned for. Nothing will interfere with the dream Arthur and myself have because we are in charge of our own destinies. You will thank me for setting you up to succeed, not to fail, and four weeks is just enough time to do that. So, clear your 'to do' list and head off to paradise because when you return, you will realise that life at the top is not as easy as you think it is."

Her phone rings and she waves her hand, effectively dismissing me, and I quickly head back to my desk. I'm not sure why I feel a little annoyed that she's appointing my replacement, but I have to bow down to her better judgement. After all, she's the successful one and it's time I learned from the master.

After work, I meet Heidi at the Cocacabana room and tell her about my plans and to say she is excited is an understatement. "Oh, my goodness, that's amazing, I am so jealous, can I help?"

Laughing, I nod happily. "Of course, I'll need all the help I can get if I'm going to make this work in the timeframe."

She screws up her face and puts her 'she means business' face on. "Right, let's get started; what's up first?"

Removing the spreadsheet I have already started to draft, I lay it out on the table. "Well, some things may require more planning than others, so here's where I'm at. I've been researching some trips away and think I've come up with the perfect one that ticks a few of the boxes."

"Where is it, oh, don't tell me, is it somewhere hot, I couldn't bear being left behind in the cold?"

"No, I doubt it's hot and actually, it's not too far as it happens."

Grinning, I decide to put her out of her obvious misery. "Camping."

The look on her face makes me laugh out loud, and she shakes her head in disbelief. "You have got to be kidding me. Since when did you think camping was a good idea?"

Shrugging, I refer to my 'to do' list and point to several items circled in red. "May I draw your attention to the following items? 10 - Dance under the stars with the man you've just kissed. 11 - Sing in the rain. 15 - Camp out under the stars. 18 - Go for a walk by the sea and gather shells and 21- Exercise. I have also added a few of my own that include cooking outdoors, keeping fit and learning a new skill. I think this little weekend trip will cross these items off my list, leaving me free to move onto the next ones."

"But where, it's January for goodness' sake? You'll freeze your knickers off."

"Maybe, maybe not."

"What's that supposed to mean?"

Suddenly, her eyes light up and she leans forward. "You're going glamping, aren't you? I'm guessing you've been on secret escapes again and found some five-star adventure experience with all mod cons and none of the suffering. I've got to hand it to you, Lily, you're good at this."

Feeling slightly annoyed with myself that I hadn't thought of this, I say matter-of-factly, "Actually no. To be honest, I feel I need to enter into the spirit of the occasion and do things properly. No, I have booked myself on the outward-bound camping experience in the New Forest at the weekend. It says not for the faint hearted and I take that to mean because it's in January. However…"

Heidi's eyes light up. "Go on, I'm dying here." She puts her hand to her mouth and looks horrified. "Oh, I'm so sorry, I didn't mean…"

"It's fine, I know it's just a figure of speech."

I smile, but inside my heart is hollow. Yes, the reason I am doing this is still at the forefront of my mind, which is giving me the courage to go through with it.

"Aunt Daisy would be proud of me because this is well and truly out of my comfort zone and, as they say, no pain, no gain. No, I have drawn up a list of things I need to purchase to make things, shall we say, a little more comfortable."

Heidi looks so excited it makes me laugh. "Go on, tell me, this is so interesting."

Feeling rather pleased with my expert planning, I withdraw my camping preparation list from my pink folder. "Right, obviously I need a tent, so I managed to purchase a Cath Kidston one in the sale. It was 70% off you know, so not only a designer's dream but an affordable one at that."

Heidi looks surprised. "I didn't know they did tents."

"They do everything a girl needs, Heidi. It's a particularly pretty one with flowers on and will brighten up any forest we find ourselves in. Now, obviously I need to transport the tent, so I managed to purchase one of those hard cases on wheels to pack it in, along with a polka dot sleeping bag and matching towel. Again, January is the perfect time of year to grab those sale bargains. You know, I even tweeted about it just this morning and had several likes and a few comments already thanking me."

Heidi is beginning to look a little worried and I laugh happily. "You know, it will be fine. I've even ordered some of those joss sticks to burn to keep the creatures away because quite frankly, I'm sharing with no one, not even an errant spider looking for shelter. No, I'll be tucked up inside my cosy tent with my happy socks firmly on my feet and a relaxing face mask to de-toxify my skin, while being at one with nature."

Heidi shakes her head and looks concerned. "I'm not sure you've really thought this through, Lily. I don't think they allow suitcases on wheels in the forest. What if you have to go off-road, or get it stuck in the mud?"

Sometimes I wonder about my friend's intelligence and roll my eyes. "Then I'll use the handle and carry it - obviously. You know, I think it's ingenious because I won't be bogged down with my home on my back like some kind of snail. No, I have planned ahead and come up with the perfect solution. The best thing is, I've also managed to order a few of those battery charger packs, so I'm covered for the duration with spare charge for my phone. You see, Heidi, forward planning is the key because now I'll be able to stay in touch with civilisation, while ticking a few of the boxes off my list. You know, as Sable once told me, an organised woman is a powerful one. Well, that's me because I'll have more power in my wheelie case than I do when I'm at home. Ingenious."

Shaking her head, Heidi changes the subject. "What else have you arranged?"

Feeling rather smug at how quickly I've risen to the challenge, I jab my finger at item number 22.

"Tomorrow morning I'm off to the Art institute to paint a naked man."

Heidi's face is a picture and I giggle. "I know, mad isn't it? Well, I called them on my lunch break and they were so helpful. They told me they had an opening at 10.30 tomorrow and when I asked how much it was, they told me £40. Well, it's a little steep, but at least I'll get this one done. Oh, I almost forgot, I love that colour on you, it brings out the um… greyish green of your eyes."

Heidi looks even more confused until I point to item number 19. "Aunt Daisy wanted to compliment herself every day, but I have changed it to compliment another. That way I'm helping spread the love and making someone's day at the same time. You know, Heidi, I really think I've got this. You see, Aunt Daisy was an impressive woman and some of it must have rubbed off on me."

Grabbing the list, Heidi reads it and by the end of it she looks quite disturbed. "Are you really going to do all these things?"

"Yes."

"What every one?"

"Every last one."

Shaking her head, she looks impressed. "Well, I can't wait to hear all about it. I've got to hand it to you, babe, you've surprised me, I never knew you had it in you."

Feeling rather smug, I carefully place my notebook and various lists inside the pink folder.

"Watch and learn dearest friend and prepare to be amazed."

♥ *8*

The Art institute is an impressive place. As I walk into the entrance hall, I am amazed at the modern simplicity of a building that's both minimalist and yet super cool at the same time. Art is everywhere and I feel as if I've had more culture in two seconds than I did the whole of last year. Why haven't I been here before? It's not far and quite frankly, I feel as if I've missed out on so much already and now it's time to play catch up.

There are a few people milling around and I sneak a look at them as they wander around looking intellectual and arty. I belong here. Yes, I'm a creative person too and I quickly snap a selfie of me by the Art Institute sign and load it to Instagram. Maybe I'll do a feature on the design element when I'm editor. Yes, Designer homes - *on a budget,* will reap the rewards of soaking up the atmosphere of a free day at this centre of learning and culture. Thinking of the money I need to pay; I imagine it's how they fund their business. Yes, free to the public but for people like me who have the yearning for learning, we contribute to keeping the doors open and enable others less fortunate than ourselves to learn for free.

Feeling quite virtuous, I head over to the little ticket window and smile graciously. "Good morning, I've come for the life Art class, I believe you're expecting me."

The elderly woman sitting behind the counter looks at me with interest. "Oh, what's your name?"

"Lily Adams."

She consults some kind of list and smiles. "Yes, that's right, you need to head for the Monet room on the third floor. Take the lift and turn right when you get there. The Monet room is three doors down on the right. Somebody will meet you there."

"Thank you. Um… do I pay now?"

Looking surprised, the woman shakes her head. "Oh no dear, there's no charge."

Feeling surprised, I move away and as I walk to the lift, I try to remember my conversation with the woman I spoke to yesterday. I'm sure she said it would cost £40. Maybe she got it wrong, then again, it could have been the lady on the door. Now I'm in a dilemma. Do I mention it and hand over the money like the honest person I am, or do I keep quiet and save myself from spending money I don't really have?"

Feeling quite flustered, I head to the Monet room and hope the answers lie within its Art-lined walls.

It doesn't take me long to find it and as I head inside, I see a couple of people sitting there reading magazines or looking at their phone. The man looks up and smiles and I nod. "Good morning."

He returns the greeting and shifts along a little on the bench he's sitting on and says with interest, "Are you here for the life class?"

"Yes, are you?" He nods as I take my seat next to him and the girl looks up and smiles. "Same. Have you ever done this before?"

"No, have you?" The girl nods. "Several times, it's good fun."

The man laughs. "I'm not sure fun's the right word in my case but it's something to do I suppose."

He holds out his hand. "I'm Richie."

"Lily."

We shake hands and the girl grins. "I'm Betty. It's nice to meet you, Lily, I hope you enjoy it."

"I'm sure I will, it's a little different for me but something I'm keen to experience."

The door opens and a rather bohemian looking woman enters and smiles as she sees us waiting. I take in her flowing skirt and tight V-neck sweater that provides the blank canvas for the multitude of beads slung around her neck. Her hair is the mad frizzy variety and her blue eyes twinkle behind the thickest glasses I have ever seen. "Good, you're all on time. That makes things a lot easier. Ok, my name's Carlotta and I should have Richie, Lily and Betty here, is that correct?"

We nod and she grins. "Good, well, the changing room is through there. You will find everything you need inside and when you're ready you can bring your things and I'll stow them in the lockers until you need them later."

She smiles and says lightly, "Any questions?"

Thinking of the money I owe, I decide to keep quiet for a while. Just until I suss this out, at least that's what I'm telling myself.

I follow Betty into the room and notice a set of cubicles along one side, with curtains across. Gosh, this is interesting. We must be changing into an artist's smock or something. Maybe there'll be a beret? I certainly hope so. Already picturing the exciting Instagram post I'll upload later, I head into the changing room. However, all I can see is a long white robe hanging on a peg and I say loudly, "Excuse me, Betty, I think I'm missing the uniform."

She pokes her head out from behind her curtain and says with confusion, "What uniform?"

"Um, the overalls or something along those lines."

Shaking her head, she says, "No, it's just the robe, that's all you need."

She pops her head back inside and I say loudly, "Just the robe, do we wear it over our clothes then?"

Richie shouts, "No, of course not. Just strip naked and the robe will cover your modesty."

Now I'm ultra-confused and hesitate as a sinking feeling washes over me. My voice shakes as I say rather hysterically, "Um... just another question, what exactly do we do when we get in there?"

Betty emerges from her changing room dressed in her robe carrying her clothes. "We just sit where they tell us and pose for the artists. It's all quite easy really, except when you need to move, or scratch your nose, they get angry if you move an inch."

"So, we're not painting then?"

Richie emerges from his cubicle and laughs out loud. "I think you've come to the wrong place, honey; we're the models and they are painting us, not the other way around."

My face must be a picture of its own because Betty and Richie share a look and then Betty says gently, "You didn't know?"

I shake my head and she says kindly, "You know, maybe you should still give it a go. It's not that difficult and we get paid well for it. I think it's £40 today because we're in the advanced class."

"Advanced class?" My voice sounds weak and nothing like the powerful woman I aspire to be as Richie nods. "Yes, at least their pictures will look like us. Last time I did a class with the beginners, I didn't recognise myself. They spent the whole time giggling and quite honestly it was getting irritating."

Betty nods. "Yes, there will be none of that today. Pure professionals who are only interested in the art. You should give it a go, Lily, it will empower you."

Maybe it's because she used words that strike a chord with me, or maybe it's because I've suddenly lost the power of rational thought but I say slowly, "Ok, I don't suppose there's any harm in it, after all, it's only two hours."

They nod with appreciation and Betty says, "Good for you, Lily. Go and get ready now before you change your mind. We'll look after you, won't we Richie?"

He nods and because it seems so normal to them it makes me relax. Yes, I can do this. I will be like Rose in the film Titanic and I'll just imagine Leonardo Di-Caprio is painting me. I will be a desirable woman with the world at her feet immortalised in Art and may even find myself hanging in this actual public gallery while the viewing public hail me as the muse that created the artist's finest works. Years from now, people will make up stories about me and I will sell for millions at auction as I knock the Mona Lisa off her perch.

Yes, she who dares wins after all and this is my calling.

Exactly twenty minutes later, I change my mind. What was I thinking?

As we head inside the room, I see the curious looks of a room full of people of all ages and gender, standing behind their easels looking interested. In the centre of the room are three chairs placed in a circle with their backs to each other. Carlotta says quickly, "Right, models. Grab a chair each and arrange yourself artistically. I'll take the robes and give them back to you at the end."

I almost can't look as Richie drops his first and strides to the furthest seat. Betty follows close behind and I find myself clutching my robe to me in pure and utter terror as I contemplate what I've agreed to. I can't do this, be naked in public. What if they laugh? What if they notice my cellulite and the fact my nail varnish is chipped on my toenails and my legs are winter hairy. I can't believe this is happening.

Carlotta looks a little confused and holds out her hand. "The robe dear, the artists are waiting."

I could back out, I *should* back out, I *must* back out but something is stopping me. It's the thought of how proud Aunt Daisy would be of me. This is surely what she meant when she wrote that list. Facing your fears and ditching your inhibitions. Surely if she could have sex with a stranger on the beach, I can do this. Thank goodness that one was ticked off, I'm not sure I'd be up for that but this…can I do it, really?

I sense the irritation mounting in the room and see Richie and Betty smiling with encouragement as they watch me with interest. They don't seem to care. They are sitting there seemingly unconcerned that their private parts are on full display. This is a professional environment and the only person with issues in here is me, so with a superhuman effort on my part, I let the robe drop to the floor and charge towards the seat and try to arrange myself in a pose that disguises my face and erogenous zones.

However, Carlotta is having none of it and proceeds to position the three of us for maximum effect. A head pulled back at an angle, arms arranged above our heads or dangling to the side. Legs open, or knees slightly bent and by the end of it, I feel as red faced as the magenta currently being mixed with some other colour on the artists palettes.

Then begins the most mortifying experience of my life, as I allow total strangers to stare at my body with a critical eye and point out with the stroke of their brushes, or a sweep of their charcoal, absolutely every imperfection I have ever had and try not to look at when I stare at myself in the mirror. This is brutality at its worst and I make a vow to never and I repeat, never, agree to anything without checking the facts first.

By the end of the session, I'm a nervous wreck. My muscles ache, which surprises me because I forgot I had any. My back is stiff and my head feels heavy. There's a draft caressing my body that makes my extremities stand to attention and there are goose bumps all over my body that are definitely not an attractive feature. My face is frozen with a mask of indifference, disguising the extreme embarrassment this has brought me and when the call comes to stop painting, I breathe a sigh of relief and almost pounce on Carlotta as she hands me my robe and says happily, "Well done, dear. Now, I'll make you all a nice cup of tea while you take a look at the artist's work."

As she heads off, I follow Richie and Betty around the room as we look over the shoulders of the very people who have painted us for the last couple of hours and if I thought I was about to see a masterpiece then I was definitely mistaken. All we see are the basic outlines of our bodies with none of the detail. Betty must sense my surprise because she whispers, "They fill in the rest later from memory. They just need us for the outline and perspective. Some of them may have taken a photograph and will use that to finish it off, others like to freestyle."

I look at her in alarm and hiss, "What, they have pictures of us, on their phone?"

The hysteria is rising and Betty smiles, "It's ok, they delete them when they finish. They must sign a confidentially agreement and aren't allowed to store the photos past the class."

"But how do you know, they may be perverts who do this for kicks? We might be added to some kind of weirdo wall in their apartment and when the police raid it, be brought in for questioning."

Betty laughs and shakes her head. "Relax, they're not interested in us, just Art."

Looking around, I try to suss out the artists, as she calls them. As I scrutinise them, I look for any signs they have an ulterior motive for being here but quite frankly, I doubt it. Most are older women who look like my mum in an artier way. The few men that are here look normal enough, not like I imagine a pervert or a stalker to look like in the slightest.

Betty whispers, "I've been doing this for months. It helps pay the bills on my student loan. Money for nothing, what's not to like?"

As we move through the paintings, I relax a little. Yes, I'm in a cultured environment at the Art Institute. These people would have been vetted and they don't just allow any random person in here. I must loosen up a little and relax. This is the new me after all. She who dares wins and I am winning at life. Aunt Daisy would be proud of me and it's that thought that settles my nerves and pushes the doubts away. At least I can tick one of my numbers off. I'm on my way.

♥9

Mum looks worried. In fact, she's never looked so worried, and that makes me feel anxious. She popped over to see me before I head off on my camping weekend and I can tell she has something on her mind.

Slamming my case shut, I say briskly, "Ok, spit it out."

"What?"

"Whatever's bothering you. I can tell something is, so you as may as well get it off your chest."

Shaking her head, she says with a slight hesitation, "Um... this list you've drawn up."

"Yes, what about it?"

"Um... it doesn't have the same, or even similar things that were on Aunt Daisy's list... does it?"

Fighting the urge to laugh out loud, I just shrug. "Maybe, maybe not, why does it matter?"

I can tell she feels uncomfortable and know exactly what she's thinking but decide to let her squirm a bit first. "It's just that, well, um, times have changed and people are a little more aware than they used to be. I mean, I expect Daisy wrote that at a time when the dangers that lurk around every corner weren't so well known."

"Like what?"

I know what she's getting at but it amuses me to see how she'll voice her concerns. "Um... like meeting strangers and engaging with them in a, you know, um… intimate way."

I just stare at her sharply and she looks a little embarrassed, then she appears to have a word with herself because she flings her hands up in the air and says loudly, "Oh, for goodness' sake, I'll just spell it out for you. Don't sleep with strangers, you don't know where they've been. Also, they could be a murderer, or a weirdo. Don't engage with anyone until you have stalked them on Facebook and discovered every last thing about them. Make sure they're a real person because I watch Catfish on repeat most days and quite honestly, Lily, it's a sick world out there. Promise me you'll be careful because we don't want any more bad news."

She looks so concerned, I feel bad and smile sweetly. "It's ok, mum, I haven't added in any sex with strangers to my list. Do you think I should?"

She stares at me in horror and I burst out laughing. "It's ok, you don't have to worry about me; I couldn't think of anything worse."

As I pull my case off the bed, she looks concerned. "Have you thought this through, darling? I'm not sure a case is the right equipment for camping. Maybe Cath Kidston do a rucksack instead."

"No way, I'm doing this the Lily Rose way. The last thing I want is a rucksack weighing me down when I have the power of wheels at my disposal. I'm sure there are paths in the forest and to be honest, I doubt we will be going rogue, anyway. I expect they have full hook up and showering facilities, not to mention a well-stocked restaurant to serve us roast dinners and soup on demand."

"Ooh, I'm not so sure, surely that would have been in the brochure."

"What brochure, I just googled camping trips and this one came highly recommended on Trip Advisor? I mean, obviously there were a few scaremongers' but you always get those. No, this is perfect because it ticks several boxes at once and then I'll be home to face my next challenge. I mean, how hard can it be?"

Mum follows me downstairs and as I start loading the boot of the car with enough equipment for a week away, she watches me looking nervous. "Take care, darling, and text me when you get there. I shan't rest unless I get my hourly messages."

Rolling my eyes, I pull her in for a hug. "Listen, just you wait and see, I'll be back before you know it. After all, I need to get back for the funeral next Wednesday. How are things going with that?"

"Ok, I guess. Your father's in his element organising. He has an encrypted file on Word that he forgot the password to and spent the whole day trying to crack the code before the vicar showed up for our hymn choices. Then he spent one afternoon calling everyone in Aunt Daisy's address book and quite honestly, Lily, there were some very shady people in there."

Now I'm interested. "Like who?"

She lowers her voice, although I have no idea why and says in a whisper, "One man was foreign, Italian, I think. He started crying when dad told him and said his heart was broken. He was quite inconsolable for a while there and then just slammed the phone down. Well, it was a bit rude but I'm not so sure it was deliberate."

"What do you mean?"

"He may have had a heart attack brought on by the shock and collapsed and died on the other end of the phone. You see, grief does strange things to a person you know. Take me for instance."

"You, you're no different than you always are."

"Outwardly, darling, but inwardly I'm in pieces. You know, the other day I missed the turning for Slater street and ended up on the one-way system. I was preoccupied with thinking about what canapes Aunt Daisy would have wanted for her funeral and it send me doolally."

"For goodness' sake, mum, you're always ending up on the one-way system. You just forget to concentrate and your mind veers off to another dimension from the rest of us. It's not grief, it's just you."

I slam the boot shut and pull her in for a hug. "It's only two days and I'll be back before you know it. Look after yourself and don't let dad drive you mad with his planning. Call me whenever you like because I have more power than the national grid in my portable charger packs."

As I kiss my mum goodbye, I feel a little bad that I'm deserting her in her hour of need. Then again, I need to get away because they are at their worst in a crisis and go into some sort of super organising mode that grates on my nerves after a while. It started with scouring the house for valuables and ended up with a full-blown military operation in planning the funeral. I've lost count of how many practice sessions we've re-enacted in the living room, so we do Aunt Daisy proud. Do people really rehearse funerals? I've never known it myself, but maybe they do these days. Next thing we know they'll be having funeral showers, or something along those lines. Thank goodness I'm out of bounds for a few days and can reconnect with my inner goddess in the wilds of the New Forest, and hopefully it comes with full hook up.

♥ *10*

I'm feeling quite smug. Not only have I embraced this challenge with an energy I never knew I had, but I have made good choices.

As I park the car in Sandy Balls car park, I look around at the picture of outdoor excellence. Yes, this is what I wanted, an outdoor home from home. Little lodges nestle among the trees and the well-maintained grounds demonstrate an attention to detail I appreciate. Well worth the money if you ask me because being tucked up in one of those wooden mansions will be no hardship. I can even see a chimney protruding from the back of one of them, indicating a warm and cosy log burner inside. Yes, Aunt Daisy would love it here and so, with a new spring to my step, I go in search of registration, making sure to leave my case in my car, hopefully to be retrieved later by a friendly porter.

As it's January, it appears quiet, but I expect it's a different place in the summer. I can only imagine the hordes of holiday makers that descend here each year in pursuit of the British dream.

As I make my way into the reception, I feel at home already as a receptionist looks up and smiles.

"Are you here for the outward-bound camping expedition?"

"Yes, I hope I'm not too early."

Check in was 10.30, but I made good time and now I'm early. She shakes her head. "It's fine. You can check in and then wait for the others in the bar. They shouldn't be long."

As I sign the registration form, I feel good about myself. Yes, I can do this. Run away and have adventures in my spare time, while juggling a high-powered job and all that comes with it.

The receptionist directs me to the bar area and I feel at home already as I sink into one of the comfy settees by an open fire and order a coffee from the agreeable waitress who races over to take my order. Using the time wisely, I take a few selfies and post them on Instagram and Facebook, making sure to get the fire and coffee in the background. I caption it, #camping and #outdoorsadventure. Almost immediately I get a few likes which settles any nerves I may have had. Yes, I will document my month of adventure to look back on when I have no time for such frivolities. Aunt Daisy had her box of photos and so must I.

Soon, I am joined by several people who look a little more rustic than me. I thought the leather look leggings and ski boots were a good choice when paired with the white fur-trimmed puffa jacket and white earmuffs. I made sure to buy those gloves that enable you to text at the same time and the mirror shades I bought from BrandAlley at a knockdown price, make me look as if I'm ready for the ski lift.

My fellow campers look a little more conservative in their waterproof trousers and walking boots. I shiver as I see the dull green and camouflage brown of their weather proof jackets and most appear to have woolly hats or beanies perched on their heads. Giving myself the prize for the most glamorous camper, I smile at my new companions as they look at me with a slightly stunned expression.

The only woman among them comes over and says in a friendly voice. "Are you here for the outward-bound camping adventure?"

"Yes, have you been on one before?"

She sits beside me and shakes her head. "No, and I must say I'm a little apprehensive."

I laugh lightly. "What's to be worried about, this place looks amazing? It will be no hardship staying here for the weekend."

She gives me a strange look and whispers, "You do know we aren't actually staying here, don't you? This is just the rendezvous point."

Feeling a little foolish, I say airily, "Of course, silly me, I'm always joking around."

I notice an array of backpacks littering the floor and shudder as I see the sheer size of the things. Congratulating myself on my forward planning, I say sympathetically, "Goodness, they look heavy. I hope you have a strong back."

Rolling her eyes, the lady laughs and holds out her hand. "I'm Felicity by the way. Us girls must stick together because if I know my James, he will take over and start issuing his orders before we've even left the car park."

Looking over at James, I see a tall, thin man, studying a map with a look of utter concentration.

Felicity laughs. "James loves all this. The harder the better. I can't believe he talked me into going with him. I mean, I would much rather stay here and wave him off, while I indulge in some 'me' time at the local spa."

Immediately, I can tell that Felicity and I will get along just fine. I notice another couple of men standing nearby and whisper, "Do you know if they're coming?"

She glances over and shrugs. "I think so, although I'm not sure why."

"What makes you say that?"

"Well, I heard them talking and think they're German or something. I couldn't understand a word they were saying."

I feel a little disappointed that there aren't more women and people to have fun with, but at least Felicity seems nice, so all is not lost.

Suddenly, we hear a loud, "Ok, line up campers, let's get started. My name is Finley Roberts but you can call me Finn and I'm your guide this weekend."

Looking around, my jaw hits the ground as I behold the rugged camping god who has just walked in. Bear Grylls move aside because it appears our instructor was born in the forest. Tall and muscular, with rugged good looks and eyes that could melt any woman's resolve from the next town. Immediately, I feel a renewed interest in the weekend and stand quickly to line up with the others.

I feel as if I'm on parade as he walks up and down and assesses us all. When he reaches me, I see a smirk on his rather handsome face, along with a look of resignation. Leaning forward, he barks, "Name?"

"Um… Lily Rose Adams, sir."

I almost salute but luckily his arrogant smirk stops me making a complete fool of myself, as he says in a husky voice that does things to me inside I forgot existed. "Why are you here?"

I feel the surrounding smirks rather than see them and pull myself up to my full height and say in a strong, she means business, voice, "For the adventure."

Shaking his head, he moves down the line and I hear him ask the same thing of everyone. When he reaches the Germans, he says something in what I can only assume is German, and they answer him in much the same way. I feel quite impressed as he has a conversation with them and then feel less impressed as his razor-sharp stare flicks back to me and he barks, "Where's your kit?"

"Kit?" I stare at him in confusion and he says slowly, "Your bag, rucksack, tent, sleeping bag; you do have them I take it?"

Feeling a little put out, I say icily, "Of course, they're in my car."

"They aren't much use in there. Go and get them and then we'll head off."

He turns to talk to James and Felicity throws me a sympathetic smile and whispers, "Do you need a hand?"

She seems kind, so I say gratefully, "Lovely, thank you."

As we walk away, she sighs. "Wow, that guy is seriously gorgeous. Trust my luck to be here with James."

"Is James your husband?"

She grins. "Not yet. We are engaged, but he appears in no hurry to make an honest woman of me."

"How long have you been engaged?"

"Ten years."

I stop in my tracks and she shrugs. "It just never seems the right time to plan a wedding. First, there was the house and the mortgage. We didn't have the money, so we used what we had to sink into bricks and mortar. Then we had to do the place up, and then James lost his job and took a while to find a new one. You know, Lily, it's ceased to be important and we have just fallen into the trap of every married couple out there. The excitement has gone and neither of us are that bothered in putting a ring on it and making something official that works without it."

We reach the car and for some reason I feel sorry for Felicity. Fancy the spark dying before they even made it down the aisle. Hardly the stuff of romance novels, but she appears happy.

As I unlock the boot and retrieve the case, her eyes widen and she laughs out loud. "What the hell is that?"

Feeling a little aggrieved, I say shortly, "The latest Cath Kidston, all terrain, hard case. Ingenious if you ask me."

I can tell she's trying hard not to laugh and pity her even more for her short sightedness. As I heave the case to the ground, I feel quite smug as I look at it standing proudly on the gravel surface and say happily, "Right, just my handbag and cosmetics case and we're good to go."

As I attach the matching cosmetics bag to the handle of the case, Felicity laughs. "You've never been camping before, have you?"

"No, this is the first time."

Shaking her head, she says lightly, "I hope you don't think I'm speaking out of turn here, Lily, but I'm not sure if the case is a good idea. I mean, it's lovely, but there aren't many hard surfaces to drag it along and the mud will choke up the wheels. I know the backpacks aren't anywhere near as gorgeous as this, but they are practical and made to do the job and do it well. This may be good for a holiday but camping – well, it requires a more basic set up and I just don't want you to struggle."

She smiles sweetly and despite the fact I feel annoyed at her condescending words, I can't be annoyed at her for trying to help, so I just shake my head and laugh. "Oh, don't you worry about me, I'm stronger than I look. Anyway, we should get going. That guide looks as if he'll come and hunt us down and rope us in or something. He seems quite scary in a rugged good-looking way, of course."

Felicity grins and we set off giggling like schoolgirls as we make our way back to the rendezvous point.

♥ *11*

"Absolutely not, no way, you are not taking that."

"Why not, I would have thought I could take whatever I want because, in case you've forgotten, I'm the paying customer and know best?"

I cross my arms and fix my most ferocious stare onto my face as I glare at the monster who has made himself in charge this weekend.

I feel the suppressed laughter around me, which only makes me dig my heels in even more and for a moment, we are two gladiators in the ring, sizing each other up, looking for the chink of weakness to bring our opponent down.

Finn looks as if he's reached the end of a very short fuse, which should make me back down but for some reason this suitcase has become the most important thing in my life, so I say angrily, "Listen, I'm not asking for help and I'm not asking your permission. This is what I'm taking - end of. If it all goes wrong, then I'm the one who will suffer – not you. So, rather than delay our expedition while we 'discuss' my portable equipment, maybe you should actually do what we are paying you to, and lead us off on our adventure."

For a moment Finn looks stunned and I see an angry tick working away in his neck. I feel quite proud of myself for standing up for what I believe in the face of extreme adversity and look around me triumphantly as he sighs and turns away, mumbling, "You've been warned and now you'll have to deal with the consequences."

He grabs his own army issue kit and says shortly, "Follow me. We have at least five hours before we make it to base camp for the night. Try to keep up."

He storms ahead and Felicity throws me a sympathetic glance as James says loudly, "Hurry up, Felicity, we can't afford to fall behind. Grab your backpack and set your step counter, we need to do in excess of 10,000 steps in the next five hours to make up for yesterday."

As she grabs her backpack, Felicity pokes her tongue out at James behind his back and salutes him mockingly. Stifling a giggle, I watch the two suspected German men hoist their own impressive looking kit on their backs and set off at an almost jog in the direction of our surly leader.

Once again, I feel smug as I pull my case effortlessly behind me as I follow them, trying to ignore the rather annoying sound of the wheels on the stone path.

As days go in January, this one seems quite a good one. I'm grateful for my shades as the sun beats down from a cloudless sky, reminding us that spring is hopefully not too far away. The ground is hard beneath my feet and I'm glad I wore the snow boots because they are comfortable and are keeping my feet warm on the rather hard ground that has been the recipient of frost during the night.

Taking a deep breath of the crystal pure air, I thank God I decided to do this. Yes, this is what I need, a detox after the shock of the last few days. To re-energise my mind and take stock of my new life. To remind myself of what's important in life and to embrace the unknown before I become a woman of status and importance in the modern corporate world.

Smiling to myself, I see a couple of squirrels playing among the trees and hear the sound of a bird above my head. The wind whips carefully around me with a cool breeze that soothes my increasingly heated body. In fact, the more we walk, the hotter I get and soon the ear muffs are deposited in my pocket as I crave the soothing cool breeze to calm my increasing temperature.

The others appear to be lost in their own thoughts as they use all their energy to keep up with our surly guide. He only looks around once in the first hour and for all he knew, we could have been abducted by wolves or fallen down a ravine. Probably ten minutes after meeting him, I decide he is definitely not my type. Sexy, yes. Good looking, incredibly. Strong, obviously. Swoon worthy, absolutely. However, all those good points are magically erased by the fact he is obviously a complete asshole. He is rude, abrupt and surly. He has no conversation and appears to lack any shred of social interaction that I would have thought was imperative for a job such as this. Surely, they could have picked a better guide than him. I thought tour guides were supposed to be fun and entertaining. I thought we'd be singing some hearty songs as we trudge through the forest, or play games designed to keep our spirits up. He obviously tore up the memo because he is decidedly rude and if I could be bothered to think anything of him at all, it would be to hate him with a passion.

We stop for a breather at the top of a hill and the view from it is breath-taking. I watch as my companions produce some kind of water bottles from their backpacks and sink down onto a grassy bank and take the weight off their feet. Once again, feeling rather smug, I lay my case down and note that it's now completely plastered in mud. Reaching into my cosmetics holdall, I take out a wet wipe and wipe my case clean before sitting on it and producing a can of red bull from my rations and sip it delicately as I take in the view.

I don't miss the envious looks Felicity throws me as James pulls her down beside him and throws her his hip flask. "Remember, Felicity, small sips only, we need to conserve our rations."

He then proceeds to consult his ordnance survey map again and points out various items on it to a bored looking other half.

The Germans are whispering to themselves, and if I knew any German at all, I'm not sure it would help me. It all sounds rather difficult to understand, so I resign myself to a lot of alone time during the next couple of days. Finn appears to be brooding about something, so I whip out my phone and take some selfies, making sure I get the stunning view in the background. Applying a filter to the best one, I load it to Instagram with the hashtag #livingmybestlife.

I catch Finn watching me with an expression of utter amazement as I tuck my phone inside my pocket and say loudly, "Well, I must say this is a real treat. I never get out to the country and now I can see what I've been missing."

Felicity looks interested. "Where are you from?"

"London."

Finn smirks and the Germans appear disinterested. James continues to pore over his map and Felicity says quickly, "Goodness, what made you decide to do this? If you don't normally leave the city, it's quite an undertaking."

Shrugging, I say sadly, "Because I've lost someone who meant everything to me and I'm doing it for her."

Felicity edges closer and I shift along and pat the space next to me on the case, which she takes gladly. "Do you want to talk about it?"

She lowers her voice and I see Finn turn away, seemingly uninterested, so I say in a low voice, "My Aunt Daisy. You know, Felicity, she was an amazing woman and if I turn out to be half the person she was, I would be forever grateful."

"I'm sorry, Lily, was it a short illness?"

"You could say that." I sigh. "She died of a heart attack in the night and for all we knew she was as healthy as you or I. I suppose that's what makes it so hard to deal with."

Felicity rubs my arm and says softly, "I'm so sorry, Lily."

Shrugging, I whisper, "You know she had this amazing list that she wrote when she was a young woman starting out."

"What did it say?" Felicity's eyes are wide as I say sadly, "I suppose some may call it a bucket list, but it was a list of things she wanted to do in life. I suppose it was her idea of what a perfect life would look like. The thing is, Felicity, she decided the most important thing was being successful, which she did big time. But it was the other stuff…"

"Rest over, grab your things, we need to push on to reach base camp."

Jumping up, Felicity says wearily, "Sorry, Lily. Maybe we can finish this conversation at base camp. I'd love to know what was on that list."

"Felicity, hurry up, Finn's already a few yards ahead."

Rolling her eyes, Felicity heaves her impossibly large rucksack onto her back and scurries after him with the Germans following closely behind. Sighing, I pick up my case and resign myself to dragging it for at least another hour, but still feel glad I brought it. It's been a little difficult, I'll admit that. Several times I've had to haul it over a tree root, or lift it over a muddy puddle while the others don't even miss a step. However, knowing all my possessions are carefully protected inside and my back won't need a chiropractor at the end of this, is reward enough for bringing it, despite the few minor inconveniences it involves.

As I follow them, I laugh to myself as I sense the annoyance of our reluctant guide. I'm guessing he thought my wheels would have fallen off by now, and I'd be forced to retreat to one of those snug little cabins. Once again, I congratulating myself on my forward planning because if it gets too much, all I need to do is phone for a cab to come and get me from base camp and take me back to woodland paradise.

Yes, this is all turning out rather well and my smug sense of personal achievement is the only companion I need as I head towards base camp.

♥*12*

As we trudge on through the forest, I am questioning every part of me that thought this was a good idea. Why on earth did I make this so hard for myself? I could have just hired one of those wooden cabins and spent the evening on the veranda, star gazing or something, while the wood burner bathed me in its warming heat, making everything good with my life.

Not this. I'm hungry, thirsty and hot. My snow boots started to rub an hour ago, and I'm sure there's some kind of massacre playing out inside them. My leather-look trousers are seriously causing me to sweat and the padded jacket that looked so white and ski-like, is now marbled with mud and leaves from the trees we pass under. Any make up I had on has now streaked down my face and the only thing keeping me going is the thought that base camp can't be far and I'll soon be tucked up in my Cath Kidston home from home after a hearty meal and a rendition of ging gang goolie around the campfire.

Two hours later, we reach a clearing and I swear my hands are now blistered from pulling the case what feels like a hundred miles uphill. I almost can't speak because all the breath in my body is now reserved for keeping me alive.

I will definitely not be taking any selfies in the next hour or so because there is absolutely nothing glamorous about this whole expedition and yet infuriatingly, our guide and the two Germans looks as if they've just taken a gentle stroll through the forest and haven't even broken a sweat.

As soon as we reach the clearing, Felicity collapses on the ground and shrugs off her backpack. "Thank goodness for that. I don't think I could have walked another step."

She consults her Fitbit and punches the air triumphantly. "10001, job done."

James looks at his wrist and appears annoyed. "Are you sure, darling? Mine is saying I've only done 9891. Yours must be malfunctioning."

Felicity just glares at him. "Maybe yours is malfunctioning. Then again, maybe you didn't take as many steps as I did. You have longer legs and cover more ground than I can. I also kept running back to chat to Lily while you stayed where you were, so theoretically, I covered more distance than you. So, James, maybe you should go for a gentle jog to catch up because it appears that I'm the winner on this occasion."

She turns away and winks at me, and I laugh to myself as I see his furious expression. One, nil to Felicity and I'm backing her all the way.

Finn says loudly, "Ok, this is it. Time to erect your tents for the night. I would suggest we make them into a circle. We don't have long before the light goes and I'm keen to establish a fire in the centre where we can cook our meals and keep warm."

He starts pointing at each of us and directing us to certain positions, and soon the area is awash in a frenzy of tent building.

I watch with interest as James takes charge and starts issuing orders to Felicity like a drill sergeant. She runs around doing as she's told and I sigh inside. I don't want that. When I find love, I want the hearts and flowers. I want the romance and wining and dining. When I commit to someone, I want us to be an equal team and to keep the flame burning high after several years together. As I see the silent fury in Felicity's eyes as James yells at her for not pulling tightly enough, I turn away.

Meanwhile, the Germans have their equipment laid out in an orderly fashion and are systematically erecting their home from home with a military precision. Taking a short time to appreciate their skill, I am rudely brought back to the moment as Finn barks, "Adams, stop gawping and start building. We don't have long and no one here has time to help you."

Feeling myself fuming, I look across and see that his own tent is almost up and just grit my teeth as I move to my case and flick the lock. I'll show him who needs help, certainly not me!

Quickly, I remove the bag containing my tent and with a quick flick of the wrist, it's up in less than two seconds. As the others look on in amazement, I secure the guy ropes with the shiny new tent pegs and thank god I bought the pop-up variety and look around with satisfaction. "Done."

I suppress my laughter as Finn just stares in complete amazement and says, "What on earth is that?"

"My tent."

"You call that a tent?"

"Actually, I do. It looks like a tent, was marketed as a tent and *is* a tent. Why, what's wrong with it?"

He stares at my rather impressive piece of kit and shakes his head and Felicity exclaims loudly, "Wow, they'll see you from space."

Feeling rather happy at my choice, I look with pleasure at the flower designed red and white creation that sparkles like the finest jewel among the roughness of nature. It's a designer's dream and I congratulate myself on a bargain from the local Millets that was closing down. It surprised me to find they were selling it at 70% off because the salesman told me people weren't interested in it. I was shocked because who wouldn't be interested in owning this little piece of pleasure? I am quite looking forward to spending a cosy night inside with my polka dot sleeping bag and matching onesie. Yes, this camping trip is full of surprise because I never expected I'd get so much pleasure out of shopping for the basic necessities I needed.

While the others work away, I put the finishing touches to my new home and after placing my case inside and arranging my sleeping bag, I sit proudly in my little piece of heaven. Deciding it would be surly of me not to offer to help out, I take a quick picture of my new home and upload it to Instagram with the caption, #outdoorslifethedesignerway.

As I crawl from my tent, I see that Finn has managed to erect his tent and looks to be creating some sort of fire in the centre of the circle.

Wandering over, I say brightly, "Can I help?"

He doesn't look up and says wearily, "I think I can manage to light a fire."

He carries on and I sit beside him and look with interest. "You look as if you've done this before."

"Obviously."

His tone is cutting but I shrug it off. "So, what made you become a tour guide?"

He looks up in surprise and I notice how startling his eyes are. They are the lightest blue, and yet his hair is as dark as the night sky. He has a rough stubble on his jawline that looks incredibly sexy, and for some reason, I change my mind about him in an instant. He's something else, and I owe it to my girlish fantasies to find a little more out about the man who appears to have been crafted from every dream I have ever had.

"Tour guide?"

He looks surprised and I shrug. "That's what you are, aren't you? I mean, we booked a night camping and you get to show us how it's done. We need you to show us the way, so you're our designated tour guide."

Shaking his head, he says through gritted teeth. "Actually, my job title is expedition leader."

I raise my eyes and he sits back on his heels and barks, "What?"

"Nothing."

"Then why the face?"

"What face?"

"The one that's making fun of me."

"You're a little sensitive, aren't you?"

"Is that what you think?"

Shrugging, I lean back and say with amusement. "Well, let's look at the facts. You are quick to judge a person based on what you see, rather than know. You form instant opinions and carry them with you without taking time to know the facts. Your way is apparently the only way, and you are not prepared to listen to any alternative. Then, when somebody tells you something you don't like, you get all narky and throw it back at them as if they don't know what they're talking about. You see, Finn, out of the two of us, I would say you are the most sensitive because you appear to get rattled by everything I do, even though I haven't actually asked you for anything. In fact, all I've done is tried to help and you just don't want to admit that you're wrong about me."

Leaning forward, he whispers in that husky voice that should be illegal on a man, "Time will tell, darlin'. If you think I'm sensitive, then you are way off the mark. The reason I judge you is that city girls like you, think they know everything but actually know nothing. You turn up here with your material ways thinking everything's a game. Well,

101

survival is no game and if I left you here for just one night on your own, all the designer frills you've brought with you wouldn't count for a thing because there's a reason we do things this way and you'll find that out the hard way."

He pulls back and I say lightly, "See, I told you you're sensitive. Well, toughen up buddy because I'm about to prove you wrong and I'll look forward to rubbing your nose and your opinion about me in your face. Now, can I get you a cup of tea? I have mint tea if you prefer, or just bog-standard English breakfast."

He looks at me in surprise as I nod towards my tent. "A rather nice little camping stove came with the ski boots; it was half price with any purchase over £50 so I kind of had to take up the offer. I think I've got enough water in my flask to heat up a few cups for everyone, and I have powdered milk and sachets of sugar if anyone takes them. Wait there, I'll be right back."

As I head off in search of the revitalising tea, I look forward to proving Finn wrong about me. I'm not stupid, I knew from the moment he laid eyes on me he dismissed me as some kind of city airhead who didn't know what she was letting herself in for. The fact he's right doesn't count anymore because now it's my mission to prove him wrong.

♥ 13

Soon all the tents are standing proudly in the dusky light and we are all sitting on makeshift seats around a roaring campfire, courtesy of our fearless leader Finn. I took great delight in sharing my tea bags and I think everyone appreciated the gesture because I note they are less frosty with me than before. As I sit beside Felicity she says loudly, "Oh, carry on with what you said before, Lily."

"What was that?"

I can tell everyone is listening and she says with excitement. "The letter your Aunt wrote to herself – you know, the bucket list. What did it say?"

Now all eyes are on me and I squirm a little and laugh nervously. "Oh, just random things, really."

"Go on, I'd love to know."

James interrupts and says sharply, "Don't be so intrusive, Felicity. Lily might not want to relay the contents of this letter."

I see Felicity's face fall and rally to her side. "No, it's fine, really."

Addressing the group as a whole, I say loudly. "The reason I'm here is that my Aunt died last week."

They all look uncomfortable and I say lightly, "It's fine. Well, obviously it's not fine but… um… well, the short story is, she wrote herself a letter when she was a young woman outlining her hopes and dreams for her life. When she died, she had achieved amazing things and certainly ticked off the things on the top of the list."

"What were they?" Felicity looks excited and I smile. "Well, numbers 1-3 were success." They look confused and I say sadly. "Yes, that was obviously the most important thing to her and to be honest, she knocked it out of the park. She was the most successful woman our family had ever known, and she was famous among the interior designer's community. She had everything she ever dreamed of, such as an amazing house, beautiful clothes, jewellery and exotic holidays. She was living the dream but there were several things on her list that remained unticked."

By now even the Germans are listening, and I wonder if they can speak English because they appear to be following every word. Even Finn looks interested in my tale, and I feel like some kind of motivational speaker as they look at me with interest. "Well, it appears that she didn't achieve some pretty important things that she wanted to and so, I've decided that I need to try and do them instead. You see, I am very much like my Aunt and have been offered a huge promotion."

"Congratulations, Lily, what is it?" Felicity's eyes shine as I say proudly, "I'm to be the editor-in-chief of Designer Homes - *on a budget*."

Felicity squeals, but the men look unimpressed. Finn just smirks and James looks a little bewildered until Felicity screams. "I love that magazine, the tips in there are amazing. Wow, I can't believe I'm sitting here with somebody famous. Quick, take a selfie of us, I can't cope."

She's not the only one because I feel decidedly uncomfortable as she totally fan girls on me. Is this what I'm to expect? I certainly hope not because I'm no different to any of the people here, so I say a little awkwardly, "Um... anyway, that's why I came here. This is one of the things she wanted to do in the letter. Camp out under the stars. In fact, this could tick several boxes off the list and I get to do it all in a couple of days."

"But why the rush, surely you have a lifetime to do the things she wanted?"

Felicity looks confused and I say sadly, "I think that's what she thought. I mean, she wasn't old when she had a heart attack and died. She was only in her early 50s and probably thought she had years ahead of her. Her job took most of her time, so she didn't get to do half the things she wanted to. Well, I have exactly four weeks before I fall down the same rabbit hole and take on a high-powered job of my own and I intend on completing the list in record time so I have no regrets in life."

Suddenly, Finn laughs loudly. "You think you're going to do all those things in four weeks and then you can tick the boxes and consider yourself happy. I'm pretty sure there was a reason she failed to do them in the first place."

Bristling with indignation, I say coldly, "Which is?"

He shrugs and throws another twig on the fire. "Because doing something properly and for it to have meaning, you need to plan things and savour them. You can't just power your way through someone else's list and think you'll gain great happiness as a result."

"Why not?"

"Because life doesn't work that way. What if you do everything on the list and are still unhappy? Would you make a new one and then another until you find what you're looking for? Doing someone else's list means nothing. If anything, I'd probably take a deep look inside myself and decide what it is I want out of life, not take the word of another as gospel."

There's an awkward silence until Felicity says loudly, "Have you got the list? Tell us what some of them are, maybe we can help."

James nudges her and says roughly, "Quiet, Felicity, don't get involved."

Reaching for my bag, I pull out the list and say sharply, "Well, for your information, I think her list is rather impressive. She knew a lot about everything my Aunt and I'm pretty sure if it's not on her list, it's not worth doing."

Felicity looks over my shoulder and gasps. "Have sex with a stranger on a beach. Wow, that one's ticked already."

All eyes turn to me and I feel my cheeks flame with embarrassment and say hastily, "Actually, that one was already ticked."

I laugh nervously, "Um... luckily."

I daren't look at the others and suddenly find the flames of the fire, and I have something in common due to the heat spreading through me right now.

Felicity laughs. "This list is amazing. Travel the world. Ooh, I'd like to do that."

James rolls his eyes as Finn laughs out loud. "What, in four weeks, you'll be lucky?"

Feeling annoyed, I snap. "Well, obviously some items may take a little longer but at least I've made a start."

"It says here paint a naked man. This is crossed off, was that you, or her?"

Felicity looks intrigued and I feel embarrassed as I say in a small voice, "Not exactly."

They all look interested, so I laugh as if it's nothing. "Well, it turned out they painted me. I kind of got it wrong and ended up being the vase of flowers as they say."

Felicity suppresses a laugh and I see Finn smirking at my embarrassment. The Germans appear confused and then burst out laughing when Finn says something in their mother tongue. James looks a little disgusted and I say quickly, "Well, if you must know it was quite liberating, actually. Obviously, once I got over my initial nerves, I found it to be a worthwhile experience. For all you know, I am hanging in a gallery somewhere being admired by all sorts."

Grabbing the list that appears to have made it around the circle at supersonic speed, I tuck it away and say quickly, "Anyway, enough about me, somebody else speak – please."

Grinning, Felicity says, "Well, I'm Felicity and I'm a tax adviser from Wigan. James, my fiancé, is also a tax advisor and we spend our free time trying to do physical activities to compensate for being desk bound most of the day. We don't have any pets or children, or hobbies really, unless you count walking in the country at the weekends. Most of our spare time is spent cleaning the house and doing odd jobs because we work during the week. We have two holidays a year, one like this and one in James's parents caravan in Whitby. We are not married and probably never will be because there is always something more important to spend the money on."

Her voice trails off and James cuts in, "Yes, everything that Felicity said but she forgot one thing."

She looks at him in surprise and he says briskly, "We share the same hopes and dreams and one day hope to retire from the civil service and journey around Britain in a camper van."

As I look at him, I notice he appears more animated than I have ever seen him before, but Felicity looks as if she's just chewed a wasp. Seeing the smug look on his face, I wonder if he knows Felicity is obviously not singing from the same hymn sheet. Even I can tell she's unhappy, and it's no wonder. Goodness, she needs a bucket list and fast.

Finn coughs and says quickly, "Well, I'm Finn, short for Finley and I spend most of my time outdoors. When I'm home, which isn't often, I live in a small village in Kent. I don't have any dependents, which is largely due to my profession. I'm here because I'm filling in for my brother who had the cheek to actually go and book a holiday with his girlfriend to Bermuda and needed me to take his place so you weren't disappointed."

His words surprise me because I thought this was his profession, but before I can ask what it is, one of the Germans leans forward and says in broken English, "My name is Ryker and this is Walter, my friend. We came to..." He turns to Finn and says something in German and Finn says, "They came to make up the numbers. They're both good friends of mine and were over here on business and at a loose end this weekend. This way you get your trip and we spend a weekend outdoors."

Before we can ask anything else, he jumps up and says quickly, "Ok, it's time to get some food. We've brought some rations and Walter, as it happens, is rather a good chef. He'll be responsible for cooking and I'd like a volunteer to help him."

Felicity's arm shoots up and James nudges her, looking annoyed. Finn nods and says, "Ok, Felicity and Walter are the chefs and James and Lily can wash up afterwards. Ryker and I will attend to camp maintenance and keep the fire burning and keep a look out."

"What for, is this um… safe?" I look around me
fearfully and Finn shakes his head. "Relax, it's not
the jungle you know, just the New Forest. The only
things likely to disturb us are the horses and cows
that wander around freely. As that's the last thing
we want trampling over us, we will need someone
to look out for them."

As everyone jumps to their feet, I follow James
and say lightly, "Well then, it's just you and me.
What do you want to do, wash or dry?"

He looks at me with pity in his eyes and says
slowly, "As you will probably realise, things are
very different out here. Firstly, there is no sink or
running water, so we need to locate an alternative
before it gets dark. Now, I suggest you look around
for a container that we can use to transport some
water here from a nearby stream, while I consult the
map to locate the nearest one."

He turns away, and I have never felt like
punching anyone so hard in my life.

Before I can even move, I feel a hand on my arm
and a voice sounding a lot gentler than I'm
accustomed to, "Here, it's a foldup bucket we use
for washing up. Take that, it should do the trick."

Looking up, I see Finn looking at me almost
normally and it surprises me how grateful I am for
just this one small act of kindness. For a second it
must show on my face because he says softly,
"Now, I know you probably have one already
stuffed in your case of many surprises, but it would
be a shame to get it wet. To be honest, I wouldn't

put it past you to have a working dishwasher in there either, but maybe this is the simplest thing for now."

He winks and then heads off, leaving me speechless. Did he just try and make a joke with me? Goodness, I must have sat too close to the fire because I'm delirious. For a moment there, I thought he was actually human.

♥*14*

I don't believe it. I've just had the best meal I
think I've ever eaten, and it was prepared for me by
a German and a tax advisor from Wigan. They have
outdone themselves because the few simple
ingredients that Walter fried up in his camping
frying pan, was as good as anything a Michelin
starred restaurant could have served.

There was even a small bottle of wine that we
divided between us all and as the fire danced in the
chill of the night and the conversation echoed
around me full of good humour and interest, I can't
remember ever feeling this happy.

James and I wash up in the little bucket, using
water boiled on the fire that we found in a nearby
stream. It is back to basics, and I can certainly see
the appeal of it now. One by one my fellow campers
retire to their tents and as I crawl into mine, I
congratulate myself on a plan coming together.

Somehow, I manage to shrug out of my now
filthy clothes and wriggle into the onesie I bought
for the occasion. Then I pull on Heidi's happy socks
and knitted bobble hat that she presented me with
the day before I came and turn to my cosmetics bag.
Quickly, I cleanse, tone and moisturise and apply
one of those paper face masks to detoxify my skin.
Then I spray around my calming lavender sleep
spray and crawl inside my polka dot sleeping bag,
before reaching for my phone and plugging it into

the first of four portable chargers that I brought with me.

As I check my texts and emails, I could be forgiven for thinking I'm tucked up in bed in my flat. I don't feel cold and it's really quite snuggly in my one-man tent with room for a wheelie case. In fact, I can use the hard shell of the case as a table and proceed to text my loved ones before turning in for the night.

The first one is to mum.

Lily

Hey, all is good and I'm safe and strangely loving the experience. I hope all is well at home and the cake you made for the vicar didn't give him food poisoning like it did the undertaker. xoxo

My next one is to Heidi and I take a quick photo of my happy sock cocooned feet and another of my masked face showcasing the bobble hat.

Lily

Hey, babe. The mission is going well. All tucked up in designer comfort, congratulating myself on another tick off the list. Just so you know, there is a seriously gorgeous guy here who will be in my dreams tonight. I'll try and take a photo of him tomorrow so you can see what I mean. Take it from me, you are not going to believe this guy. Seriously, I could tick several boxes with him, if you know what I mean! xoxo

I add a winking face emoji and a heart and check my Instagram feed. I am pleasantly surprised to see I have five new followers, and as I check out their profiles; it amuses me to see they are the camping sort. This is great, I'm now tapping into a whole new audience, which makes me think a feature on designer camping on a budget may not be such a wild idea.

After enjoying a few random Facebook posts, I decide to try and get some sleep because to be honest, all this fresh air has knocked me for six. My arms are aching from pulling the case and my feet haven't stopped throbbing. Luckily, I had a tube of antiseptic cream in my emergency first aid kit and I smeared it all over the cuts and blisters those stupid snow boots caused. I think I drift off to sleep with the promise of seriously investing in some designer walking boots if I ever do this again. I wonder if Cath Kidston do them?

I'm not even sure what time it is when I hear sounds coming from outside the tent. They seep into my subconscious as I sleep and rouse me from a lovely dream where I'm leading an expedition in space with Finn as my assistant. I can hear a rustling noise coming from outside my tent and freeze in fear. Something's out there!

My heart starts beating furiously and I think I'm hyperventilating. I daren't move in case I alert whatever it is to my presence and they go in for the attack. It's pitch black outside and despite the many layers I have on, I am freezing and my teeth start chattering. The ground now feels cold and hard beneath me, and I wonder if this was such a good idea. I mean, surely this can't be good for me. Maybe I've done irreparable damage to my body by exposing it to the elements in this foolhardy way.

The rustling continues and then I hear a low moan coming from outside, which makes the hairs on my neck stand to attention. It's almost primeval and I suddenly realise I have put myself in grave danger in pursuit of adventure. Thinking of my warm and cosy bed back in London, I berate myself for ever thinking this was a good idea. Now I can see why this remained unchecked on Aunt Daisy's list – she had more sense than me.

The rustling noise appears to subside a little, but the moans intensify and my teeth start chattering. This is too much, I can't bear it, anything could happen to me out here.

Deciding some form of action is required, I quietly unzip my sleeping bag and shiver as the cool air bites me. Grabbing my phone, I turn it to torch and fumble for the zip on the door of the tent. I need to get help, that much is evident. Safety in numbers as they say, and I will not go down without a fight.

The sky is totally black, with not even a sliver of a moonbeam to light my path. The only light is from my torch and I feel strangely annoyed. So much for camping out under the stars. This is a disaster.

Once again, I hear moaning and it spurs me into action and I head towards Finn's tent because he is definitely who I need right now. He will know what to do, and even the thought of his angry expression as I disturb his sleep doesn't deter me.

Shivering uncontrollably from cold and nerves, I stumble past the glowing embers of the fire towards his tent and hover outside, suddenly unsure about my plan.

What if he attacks me, thinking I'm an intruder? That would be the last straw because this trip is not turning out remotely how I thought it would. However, another low moan propels me into action and I hiss, "Finn, are you awake?"

I hear a muttered curse and my teeth chattering are the only sound as the zip starts to move upwards and then I hear "Good god, what the hell are you wearing on your face?"

I quickly realise I still have the sleeping mask on and rip it off in embarrassment as Finn pretends to be afraid and says, "No, put it back on, it's too much."

Glaring at him, I feel annoyed that in an emergency all he can do is insult me and I say in a cross whisper, "Shut up and listen, I think we're under attack."

Suddenly, he snaps to attention and his eyes narrow and he hisses, "What is it?"

Crouching down, I lean towards him and whisper, "Something's outside my tent and there's a moaning sound, do you think it's animals?"

We listen and then the sound hits us again and Finn laughs softly, "I don't think you have anything to worry about."

"Why?"

He nods toward Felicity's tent and whispers, "They've been at it for ages. I'm surprised you didn't notice before."

Suddenly, it dawns on me what the noise is and I stare at him in shock as he grins and shakes his head, "Seriously though, what on earth are you wearing?"

Looking down at my onesie and happy socks, I shrug. "Suitable attire for sleeping outdoors, or at least I thought it was."

By now I feel as if my whole body must be blue because I have never felt so cold and Finn must notice because he says gruffly, "You're frozen solid. Here, come inside and I'll warm you up."

I stare at him in shock as he reaches for my hand and winks. "It's ok, just basic survival skills. Body heat is the best form of natural heating there is, oh and the fact I have an actual sleeping bag that's designed for extreme conditions. Not the pretend designer variety you've probably bought that looks good with no substance behind it."

As he pulls me inside his tent, I feel indignant and hiss, "Is that what you think I am, good looks but no substance?"

Trying not to laugh, he whispers, "I never said you were good looking."

Feeling very annoyed, I almost storm off but the sudden blast of heat that hits me as he unzips his sleeping bag, calls to my inner survivor and without a care for moral decency, I jump in with him with no further delay.

Strangely, I like the fact that his arm settles around my shoulders and pulls me close to his warm, male body. I love the fact I feel secure and safe in his strong muscular arms. It feels good having someone care for me when it feels so lonely out on my own, and as we snuggle down together, it feels like the most natural thing in the world.

Another moan makes me giggle and Finn laughs softly. "Maybe they've taken your list to heart and made their own one. They've certainly been giving it their best shot for the last thirty minutes."

"Do you think they know we can hear?"

"Probably not, they are too distracted."

I start to giggle as the moans intensify and Finn says, "Seriously though, what's with the Hannibal Lecter mask? I thought my time was up for a minute back there."

"If you must know, it was a detoxifying face mask that rejuvenates your skin while you sleep. Don't knock what you don't understand."

"And the hat? That's something else entirely, it kind of matches the socks which are seriously weird by the way."

"My friend made them, so it would be rude not to wear them."

"It's rude to wear them if you ask me."

"Nobody is asking you, so shut up."

The warmth from his body is so comforting, and despite my better judgement, I snuggle in a little more and don't even care that this man is technically a stranger. Maybe this is what Aunt Daisy did when she met the stranger on the beach. Suddenly, I stiffen up and Finn says, "What?"

"Um… nothing, but, um… maybe I should go back to my tent, you know, I'm sure it's safe now."

Turning to face me, Finn's eyes sparkle in the darkness and his arrogant smirk makes me hitch my breath as he says in a low voice, "You're over thinking this."

"What?"

"This, being in my tent with me."

"No, I'm not."

"Yes, you are. You suddenly realised you're in a stranger's makeshift bed and now you're thinking about that list you appear to be basing all your decisions in life on."

"Don't be ridiculous, of course I'm not thinking about the list."

"Out of interest though, what else is on it?"

Seeing Finn up close and looking so incredibly sexy and masculine is interfering with my rational thought, so I turn onto my back and look up at the canvas ceiling and whisper, "Oh you know, the

119

usual stuff, dancing in the rain, singing in a crowd, boring stuff really."

"Are you sure?"

"What about?"

"That it's all boring. I mean, I saw Felicity's face when she read it. By the looks of it there was some inspiring stuff in there, judging from the effect it had on our conservative friends."

Thinking of the racier elements of the list, I feel myself almost reach boiling point inside and squirm a little. My voice is high even to my own ears as I say with a nervous laugh, "No, nothing out of the ordinary, quite boring really, maybe not even worth considering."

A loud piercing scream, followed by a deep, almost primal, groan, cuts through the air, followed by a giggle and Finn laughs. "At last. Maybe we can get some sleep now."

Reaching out, he pulls me into him and as his arms wrap around me and pull me tight, he whispers, "Sleep well and just for the record, this is purely a survival tactic, nothing more."

I don't answer him because I don't trust the sound of my own voice right now. I have never felt so comfortable in my life, and I don't even care that I'm technically sleeping with a stranger under the stars that are well hidden under a bank of cloud because this should be on everyone's bucket list.

♥*15*

Voices wake me in the morning, and for a moment I forget where I am. As the realisation hits me, I feel the shame wash over me. I slept with a stranger. Me. Lily Rose Adams slept with a stranger and thought nothing of it. The fact that the stranger's arms are still firmly encircled around my fleecy body is a little awkward. It's also awkward to hear voices outside because the sight of me emerging from our fearless leader's tent in knitted and fleecy finery is sure to raise a few eyebrows. Coupled with the fact it's out there in black and white that this is on my 'to do' list, I almost hyperventilate with mortification.

The stranger's arms tighten around me as I try to shift away, and as my full senses come back to me, I am surprised to find I'm in no hurry to leave. In fact, this feels so warm and cosy. Finn was right. Body heat is a lifesaver in the wilderness in January because I certainly don't feel as if I've slept outside.

Finn stirs behind me and whispers in my ear, "Morning Adams."

I just manage to squeak whisper, "What are we going to do?"

"About what?"

"This. Me in your tent. I can't go out there and face the others, they'll think we… you know."

Finn laughs softly and I whip up my hand to cover his mouth. "Shh, they'll hear you. Think of something because my reputation as Editor-in-Chief of Designer Homes - *on a budget*, is at stake and I am definitely not *that* kind of girl."

Finn appears to be finding this whole situation very amusing and doesn't appear to be bothered at all, and then we hear deep guttural German voices outside. Finn answers, sounding almost the same as the German who spoke and then I hear footsteps walking away.

"What did you say?"

"I told them to give us a minute, we weren't done yet."

I open my mouth to protest extremely loudly and this time his hand covers my mouth and his eyes twinkle as he whispers, "Relax. They were just telling me they're going for a morning run. Apparently, they are the only ones up, so the coast is clear."

Moving his hand away, I whisper, "Are you sure, maybe you should go out there first."

Rolling his eyes, he unzips the sleeping bag and in one swift move, rolls me over so I am where he was sleeping. Then he winks as he grabs a warm fleece and his jacket and crawls out of the tent.

Watching him leave is a strange feeling. On the one hand, I would like nothing more than for us both to stay where we are, but then again, I am in an extremely embarrassing situation and need his help and the sooner the better.

Almost immediately, he taps the roof and whispers, "Clear."

Quickly, I scramble out and without looking back, run for my tent in all my knitted glory. Just as I reach the entrance, Felicity emerges and says in surprise, "Oh morning, Lily, you're up bright up and early."

As she rubs the sleep from her eyes, she looks at me in astonishment and says quickly, "Um... nice onesie by the way."

"Oh, this old thing. Yes, it's recommended in campers weekly as an add on to your sleeping bag. It also enables you to do your stretching exercises before getting dressed for the day."

Quickly, I start stretching from my waist and then to my toes in the vain hope that she believes a single word that comes out of my mouth.

Out of the corner of my eye, I see Finn laughing and quickly say, "Ok, all done, must get back inside and change. See you in ten."

As I crawl into Cath Kidston paradise, I groan and fall on my now freezing, damp sleeping bag. Why am I such an idiot?

Luckily, my hard case has kept my belongings dry and I quickly select a warm pair of leggings and some thick walking socks. I shiver as I quickly change into a polo neck jumper and then pull an Arran jumper over that, before shrugging on my ski jacket and thick snow boots. Then, for an extra layer of warmth, I wrap the sleeping bag around me and attempt to do something with my hair. Luckily, I managed to bring a mirror with me and justified it as a means of lighting a fire if the need arose. I've watched films where they do just that and feel quite proud of myself for remembering it.

Feeling slightly annoyed, I see that the mask obviously didn't do what it said on the packet because I look haggard and drawn. Quickly, I remove my makeup from the case and apply liberal amounts in an attempt to make me look human again. Before I join the others, I quickly check my phone and see mum and Heidi have returned my texts. The first was mum.

Mum

Good to hear from you, although one text in 24 hours is almost grounds for a missing person's report. Don't you worry though, you keep on having fun and adventures while your mother dies a slow, painful death from worrying about you. Talking of death, things are hotting up at our end. The funeral's been put back by two weeks!!! Yes, you read that right, two weeks!!! Because they won't release the body due to the sudden death verdict. Well, I told your father they may suspect murder, but he laughed at me. Yes, actually laughed at me for voicing what everyone's thinking. Anyway, text, or perhaps remember you can actually call someone and I'll fill you in properly.

PS: Please reassure me there are no strangers to be ticked off that infernal list of yours. I'm your mother – I worry. xxx

Goodness, murder! Surely not. Who would murder Aunt Daisy? All sorts of things go through my mind as I think about mum's text. Maybe it was a jealous lover – the Italian, perhaps? Maybe he didn't just slam the phone down and die; he could be on the run as we speak. Maybe he's a member of the mafia. Possibly the Godfather himself and Aunt Daisy's death was the work of a hit man. Gosh, I need to get home and fast.

Trying to distract myself, I read Heidi's text.

Heidi

For goodness' sake, text me the picture already. I am so jealous. Why do you get to have all the adventures while I run knitting for the under-fives? It may be a good money earner but my sanity is surely worth more than this. Saskia Smithson stuck a needle up her nose and needed an ambulance. I can't deal with the reports I now need to fill in and the mother is blaming poor supervision. The fact she was next to her at the time doesn't seem to count. Oh no, I should have followed you and given myself a break from the crazy people that live around here.

Love you xx

PS: I hope the hat and socks came in useful. I'm working on a vest for you next.

Quickly, I dash off some replies before I can even think of breakfast.

125

The first is to mum.

Lily

Don't panic, I'm sure it's not murder just a precaution. At least it gives us more time to rehearse for the big day. Any luck with the gospel choir yet? Also, I had a thought and smoked salmon blini with mustard jus are quite in fashion at the moment. Maybe you can suggest that to Francois from the pink squid when he draws up the menu? Got to go, need to head back to civilisation, and I need to extricate myself from under this stranger. Love you xx.

Grinning to myself, I text Heidi.

Lily

No update on the photo yet, but guess what – I did the walk of shame this morning in your happy socks and knitted hat? How's that for news! Yes, yours truly spent the night in the arms of the hottest man on the planet, and there wasn't a knitting needle in sight. There are now many ticks on the bucket list, so mission accomplished. Home soon, we can catch up then.

Love you xx

PS: You may want to hold on the vest, I think my camping days are over.

Making sure to plug my phone into the portable charger, I take a satisfied look around my orderly space and venture outside in pursuit of breakfast and that photo I now need more than life itself.

♥*16*

The atmosphere is different today. Everyone seems more relaxed, and as we sit around in our little circle it feels much more friendly than before. James is positively beaming and is chatting away to Finn about compass directions and Felicity whispers, "You know, that bucket list idea is seriously good. It got us thinking and we drew up one of our own."

I say nothing but giggle inside as I know they've made a start already. Instead, I look interested. "What have you written?"

"Well, the first one was ticked off last night." She shifts closer and whispers, "Sex outdoors among strangers."

I almost spit the tea that Finn made me across the campsite as she grins. "Good one, hey. You know, I've never seen James this animated. You should see the ideas he's had, well, it will keep us busy at the weekends, that's for sure. We may even have to include a Friday night in the diary of events."

"What else?" Now I'm interested because it appears their list is going to make mine seem tame in comparison.

She giggles and looks around furtively, before saying, "Skydiving, mountain climbing, sailing and scuba diving. Those were James' ideas, of course."

She rolls her eyes and then says excitedly, "Mine were much more romantic. For instance, I want to

128

eat ice-creams on a gondola in Venice. Sing loudly at the top of the Eiffel tower. Snog in the back row of the movies and run through the tulip fields in Amsterdam."

She looks a little wistful as she whispers, "I also told him I want to get married on a sandy beach in paradise." Shrugging, she looks down and says in a small voice, "We may have to wait for that one."

Reaching out, I squeeze her arm and say reassuringly, "It will happen. Have faith in your relationship, it will all work out in the end."

She nods and then smiles mischievously. "Anyway, I detect a slight thawing in the temperature between you and our luscious leader. What happened during lights out?"

Trying extremely hard to act normal, I shrug. "Nothing."

"Are you sure, I mean, he *is* looking at you every five seconds, something's changed?"

"No, he's not." I quickly look in his direction and instantly find myself staring into his eyes from across the circle and look quickly away. "That was just a coincidence."

"No, it's not. He can't stop looking at you this morning. Something happened, you can tell me, it won't go any further."

"Ok, everyone pack up, we've got distance to cover if you want to sleep in your own beds tonight."

I try to ignore the wink he throws me and just pray Felicity never noticed because that couldn't have been more obvious.

Jumping up quickly, I almost run to my tent and at a breakneck speed, pack all my belongings and squash down my tent, cramming it into the case, knowing that as soon as I open it the tent will pop right out again.

However, I am still glad I brought the suitcase because even though I know it's unlikely to be of any further use, it has been a lifesaver this weekend and worth every discounted penny I spent.

As expected, Walter and Ryker are packed up efficiently and well before the rest of us, and I see them deep in conversation with Finn. Nudging Felicity, I whisper, "I still can't make them out. Do they speak English at all because I'm sure they understand us but never actually say anything except to Finn or each other?"

She shrugs. "James said Finn told him they all work together. I'm not sure what they do, but James mentioned it had something to do with public relations."

"Interesting. I wonder who they work for? You know, I know a lot of the big PR firms in London, maybe I'll find out which one they work for and use them on our account. Who knows, I may even end up as Finn's client or something? I would quite like bossing him around for once."

I turn away because I can't bear the knowing smirk on Felicity's lips. Ok, it's true, I am actually quite interested in Finn since last night – who wouldn't be, but that's how it's going to stay – an interest. I have no time for romantic involvement in my new brave world, so I push any feelings I may have developed for the fearsome one aside and wait to follow orders.

For most of the day we appreciate the joys that the New Forest brings. Beautiful landscapes that spread for miles housing all sorts of wandering livestock. I take many photographs of sweet little donkeys and horses and even some cows and goats to add variety to our southern safari. I even manage to get a group photo and make sure Felicity takes one with me and Finn, which I instantly send to Heidi and look forward to seeing the jealous waves roll back towards me like a tsunami when she receives it.

For once James is entrusted with leading us and armed with his compass and bearings, he ropes Felicity in to be his assistant – as usual, leaving me and Finn to walk together for the first time.

"That suitcase is seriously irritating me."

"You're seriously irritating me."

"Good."

We grin at each other and I have to admit the case is a little annoying. The noise the wheels make is spoiling the sounds of nature all around us and drones on in the background as we forge forward towards civilisation. After a while, he stops and says desperately, "Ok, one-time offer. Let me carry the damned thing for at least five minutes, so we can enjoy some peace and quiet and before you get all uppity, I'm doing it for my own sanity."

Actually, I wasn't going to protest because the sooner I never see this case again is not soon enough for me, so I roll my eyes and hand it over. "If you insist."

Effortlessly, he lifts the case and the welcome reprieve from the noise it makes causes me to relax almost immediately.

We hang back a little and Finn says with interest. "So, what's next on the list?"

"I don't know, really. I need to go home and get organised. I also need to see my family to find out if Aunt Daisy was really murdered or not."

"Murdered, you're kidding."

He sounds shocked and I laugh. "As if. It appears they won't release the body until the cause of death is determined. Apparently, it was a heart attack, but there could have been foul play. I told mum it was just procedure, but she is imagining all sorts, so I'll need to get home and reassure her."

Laughing, Finn shakes his head. "Your mum sounds a lot like you."

"I hope not, she's mad."

There's a brief silence and then I say with resignation. "Ok, I'll admit it, yes, we are alike. However, even I know Aunt Daisy wasn't murdered because anybody who ever met her loved her and would never want to harm her in any way."

"Are you sure about that?"

"Yes, of course I am. Honestly, you're as bad as my mother. Anyway, what about you, I heard you're in public relations?"

"Sort of."

"Explain."

"No."

"Why not?" I stare at him in surprise and he grins cheekily. "There's nothing to tell. I do sort of work in public relations, it's true but you wouldn't understand and I can't be bothered to explain."

Feeling slightly miffed, I speed up and say tightly, "Fine be like that. If you won't tell me about yourself, then I'll keep my list to myself."

Laughing, he pulls me back and feeling his hand on my arm stops me in an instant. Leaning down, he whispers, "That list of yours, anything I can help you with?"

His eyes sparkle and feeling his breath on my face makes me lose my mind for a moment. He leans closer and I suddenly have an image of kissing this gorgeous man in the middle of the New Forest and it's not an unpleasant one. However, I quickly remind myself that he is an annoying idiot and shake my head. "No, nothing I can think of."

He shrugs and pulls away, leaving me feeling a little disappointed that I messed up the moment because the more time I spend with Finn, the more I like him and my angry words and nonchalant attitude is the usual way I operate when I like someone. I build an invisible wall between us to keep my heart from hurting and retreat into myself with tales of imaginary Kevin to drive the point home. However, this time Kevin is not invited because even hinting that I have a boyfriend to Finn, imaginary or otherwise, is something I am reluctant to do. I wonder why?

We stop for lunch at a traditional pub about an hour away from Sandy Balls, and as we sit by the roaring fire in civilisation at last, I feel a little discombobulated. Seeing Finn laughing with the Germans, I wonder about him. He's certainly very private and a man of many talents, but he doesn't like to speak of himself in any way. With every passing hour, I'm conscious that we will soon part company and probably never see each other again, and it's worrying me. I *want* to see him again. I've kind of got used to his annoying teasing and he makes me feel safe and secure. Maybe Finn is the man I was always meant to find, but maybe he already has a woman he goes home to. As the thought hits me, I'm suddenly jealous of the obvious supermodel that must be waiting for him in his village in Kent. It's not fair, why do some girls have all the luck? I bet she's pretty, clever and homely in a sexy way. Yes, I expect she's waiting for him now in nothing but a cotton apron with her homemade buns on display, waiting for him to sample them. Why don't I ever get a break in life and meet someone like Finn? The fact that I just have escapes me as I spiral into a fit of jealously over something I know nothing about.

Jumping up, I say awkwardly, "Um... sorry, I just need to freshen up."

I move away quickly to try and settle my out-of-control imagination. This is all too much and I need to get a grip. He's my tour guide, nothing more, and I need to remember that.

Splashing some water on my face, I try to cool down. I know the fire is hot, but that's not responsible for the heat burning me up inside causing an ache in my heart. It's the thought that in a couple of hours I will walk away from potentially the man of my dreams to exist in a corporate world alone and successful. Is this what Aunt Daisy regretted? Did she have an encounter with the Italian perhaps and chose to sacrifice her happiness for success?

Gripping the side of the basin, I stare in the mirror at the reflection of a woman on the emotional edge. I need to remember that grief does strange things to a person, and I'm not thinking rationally. Taking a few deep breaths, I reason with myself and give myself a dressing down. Yes, it's the job that matters now because that will give me the most fulfilment. There will be many more Finns in my life, but there is only one shot at the big time and it's that thought that accompanies me out of the toilet and into the small hallway leading to the bar.

♥*17*

When I return, Finn is chatting to Ryker and Walter and James and Felicity are nowhere to be seen. Taking my seat again, I try to look busy with my phone to disguise the fact that I'm sitting alone with no one to talk to.

Heidi has sent the expected reaction using a gif showing her complete and utter jealousy with the message,

Hurry home immediately we need to talk!

Mum has also sent me a WhatsApp picture of three coffins with the caption, *tell me which one you prefer in order of preference.*

Quickly, I put my phone away because the last thing I want to do is contemplate coffins as if I'm choosing a random item for the home. Honestly, why can't my mother just be normal and go with the suggested one from the undertakers?

Finn slides into the seat beside me and smiles. "So, you made it through. I've got to hand it to you, you're tougher than I thought."

"I know."

"Know what?"

"You thought I was one of them, you know, some airhead who woke up one day and thought it would be super fun to go camping."

I roll my eyes to disguise the fact that actually it was like that.

"Maybe. You certainly looked to be one when you turned up with totally unsuitable clothing and a wheelie case of all things. I was in two minds whether or not to give you an immediate refund on the spot and leave you behind."

"Why didn't you then?"

I look at him with curiosity and then it's as if all teasing goes out of the conversation because his eyes soften and he smiles sweetly. "Because you looked like fun and intrigued me."

"I intrigued you." I say it with some surprise because I've never thought of myself as intriguing before. To be honest, I'm like an open book most of the time and wear my heart on my sleeve. Maybe I'm now intriguing because of my promotion. Perhaps my inner pheromones have changed with responsibility, and I am wafting them through the air as I pass. Me, intriguing, I kind of like that.

He nods towards my phone and says softly, "Maybe we should swap numbers, who knows, I may be running another camping trip and could let you know?"

"Hmm, maybe we should. Although I thought this was your brother's business. What happened, did you enjoy ordering us all around so much you now want to make a career of it?"

Finn laughs and pulls out his phone. "Come on then, if you tell me yours, I'll tell you mine."

As we swap numbers, I feel my hands shaking a little. This is a moment to treasure, and I am not taking it lightly. A gorgeous man who is better than anything I could have dreamed up actually wants my number and I'm excited to see what happens next.

One of the Germans says something and Finn laughs and nudges me. Looking up, I see a red-faced Felicity following a worried looking James who says shortly, "Um… I think it's best we make a move. I mean, we don't want to be travelling back to Wigan in the early hours."

He scrambles for their things and says quickly, "Hurry up, Felicity, we have no time to waste."

Finn grins and jumps up and I look at Felicity with concern.

Leaning down, she pretends to grab her bag and whispers, "We were just caught in a compromising position in the men's toilets. We've been asked to leave and now we're barred for life."

She stifles a giggle, and I look at her in amazement as she scurries off after her almost husband.

The Germans are grinning and Finn is saying something to them which makes them all dissolve into hysterics. I find it quite fascinating to watch and wonder what on earth they do for a living because this whole friendship thing is weird if you ask me?

Finn takes charge once again and I follow the others, hoping that it isn't far to walk back. As I pull my case after the others, Ryker drops back and says in broken English. "We like meeting you, Lily."

"Oh, thank you, same."

He smiles and I say slowly, "When-are-you-going-home?"

"Tomorrow."

I'm not sure what else to say really because I don't want to rattle off words he doesn't understand, but he speaks instead.

"Your list."

I feel my face start to redden as I nod. "Yes."

"Make sure you finish."

"What the list?"

He nods. "Life is – how you say – short and no regrets."

Nodding, I smile sadly, "You are right, Ryker. No regrets."

Holding out his hand, he takes mine and shakes it vigorously. "You come to Germany one day."

"I would love that, I mean, one of the items is to travel the world, after all."

He winks and nods to the case. "Allow me."

Before I can answer, he lifts my case as if it's a feather and strides off after Walter, leaving me running to catch up. Finn looks around and laughs. "I told you that case was annoying. I knew Ryker would snap by the end of it."

"What do you mean, he's being a gentleman?"

"If you say so." He says something in German and the two men laugh and Finn grins. "I rest my case."

"Firstly, you don't have a case – I do and secondly you rest nothing because they could have said anything. Honestly Finn, you really are a super-charged idiot, do you know that?"

He nods and we share a smile because despite our teasing, we both know there is something developing between us that could be the stuff of dreams. The trouble is, we don't have much longer before we both return to our worlds and life takes over.

Almost as if he's thinking the same thing, he turns to James and says loudly, "James, you can lead for the final hour if you want."

James pulls himself up and says proudly, "I would be honoured, sir. Come on, Felicity, we need to get in front to lead the way."

Studying his compass, he ups his pace and Ryker and Walter fall in behind them. I look at Finn in surprise and he winks. "Let's tick one of those items off your list."

"Which one?"

My heart is beating so fast I think I'm about to pass out as Finn says, "Do something spontaneous."

"Like what?"

Raising his eyes, he reaches out and pulls me tightly against him and leans down, whispering, "Kiss the man who annoys you the most goodbye."

For once I am lost for words, as I stare into those bright blue eyes that are sparkling with the promise of something I would kill to experience. Nodding slowly, I watch his lips move towards mine almost as if in slow motion and I can't believe my luck. As they touch, he tightens his hold around my waist and pulls me closer and as his tongue entwines with mine, I taste something I've been looking for all my life. Love. As I close my eyes and enjoy the sweetest kiss of them all, the tears aren't far away. As the cold hard ground ceases to bite and the chill in the air soothes rather than freezes, I experience something so magical I doubt anything else will ever measure up to it. Time no longer has meaning because this kiss could last forever for all I care, it feels intimate, familiar and as if it was meant to be and is singularly the most romantic moment in my life.

It's also bittersweet because he said goodbye. We both know this a fleeting moment that will be caught up in daily life and evaporate into the air of reality.

I try everything to prolong the kiss because if this is the memory that I will call upon in my darkest days, I want it to last forever.

However, it has to end and so, reluctantly, we pull away and Finn brushes a stray piece of hair from my eyes and smiles. "It was a pleasure to contribute to your list Lily Rose Adams. Maybe we will meet again someday, I certainly hope so."

I don't trust myself to speak and he takes my hand and says softly, "Come on, we should catch up with the others."

As I look up, I can just about see them in the distance and say with surprise, "Goodness, did they take up running or something?"

Finn laughs. "Come on, let's tick another of those boxes, the one that says to exercise. I'll race you."

As he starts to run, I feel my inner Olympian spring to attention and I race after him as if I'm in the 100m. However, despite the fact he's carrying what must the weight of a large man on his back, he is still faster and when we reach the others looks no different, whereas I look as if I need an ambulance and an air one at that.

When we reach Sandy Balls, as expected, real life takes over and we say our goodbyes with a mixture of relief and sadness. After swapping numbers with Felicity, I make my way towards my car, dragging my mutilated suitcase behind me. It's only been two days but feels like a lifetime. My heart is now heavier than my case because as soon as we got back Finn was called into the office and the Germans headed straight off. I hung around for a while, but then even I had to admit defeat and head back to my car.

I never really got to say goodbye and I hope I'll see Finn again one day because there's a lot of promise in those bright blue eyes and I am now ruined for any other man – forever.

The best thing about going away is coming home and after a long bubble-filled soak in the bath and three cups of tea and a bacon sandwich, I almost feel human again.

The sheer number of texts from my mum make her my first port of call, but it was the promise of a roast dinner that sealed the deal.

"I thought you'd never return."

Mum swamps me in a hug in her usual over dramatic style as soon as I push my way inside the front door.

Dad shakes his head and grins and then hugs me equally hard and says softly, "It's good to see you, babe."

"It's only been a few days, goodness, you make out as if I've been on a round the world cruise or something."

Mum shrugs. "It feels like it, God only knows the stress I've been under since this whole sorry business ruined my life."

Dad rolls his eyes, "Over dramatic as always."

Looking annoyed, mum snaps, "I'm sorry David, but this is no laughing matter. We now have a murder case to deal with and time is running out. Your poor sister is hovering between Earth and Heaven, and her poor soul can't be laid to rest because of red tape. I'm at my wits end because as usual, I'm the one whose shoulders the burden falls onto."

Dad reaches out to hug her and says gently, "I know it's been a lot to deal with, but you must learn to say no and to delegate. There are several of us to do our bit, just don't be afraid to ask."

Mum sniffs and then pulls away, saying quickly, "The dinner's burning while I stand here gossiping, come through, Lily and tell me all about your camping trip."

As mum works away in the kitchen, I wash and wipe up and fill them in on my travels, minus the night spent in Finn's tent, of course. It sounds dodgy even in my thoughts, let alone if I say the words out loud.

After a while, the conversation returns to Aunt Daisy and mum says sharply, "Well, I'm leaning towards it being murder."

Dad shakes his head. "Only because you've been binge watching Miss Marple ever since they delayed the death certificate. Honestly Sonia, it was a heart attack, nothing more. Just a freak of nature and a very sad one at that."

"Nonsense, David. Nobody aged 50 just dies of a heart attack one night."

"Actually, mum, they do. All the time as it happens."

"Well, not in this family they don't. No, I'm still leaning towards the Italian. I'm guessing he engineered the whole thing and is probably named in her will as the beneficiary. You mark my words, it will all come out in the end."

"Honestly mum, your imagination is out of control."

I stare at her in shock and a hint of disapproval filters into my voice. "For all you know, Aunt Daisy may have been madly in love with this Italian and their love was unrequited. Maybe he has ties in Italy and she was so ambitious she wouldn't give up her life here for love. I'm guessing that's more like it, what does nan think?"

Dad laughs out loud. "You two are both the same. Looking for the extreme when the truth is, Aunt Daisy had a heart attack one night and died. Nothing else, no sinister plot, no unrequited love because if I know my sister, if she wanted something nothing got in her way."

Mum shakes her head sadly. "I hope so, really I do. I hope it was natural causes because at least she wouldn't have known anything about it. It must be terrible dying alone, I can't think of anything worse."

We all fall silent as it hits us again. The wave of grief that reminds us someone we love is now missing – forever.

My phone rings interrupting the moment and I pounce on it eagerly but feel a little disappointed as I see its Sable calling. Moving away from my parents, I say brightly, "Hey, Sable, how can I help you?"

She sounds distracted as she says quickly, *"Oh, sorry to disturb you on annual leave, Lily, but I'm so inundated with interviews for your replacement and the Château, I'm drowning in other stuff. Anyway, if you don't mind, I wondered if you could do one of my social engagements for me. Quite honestly, I don't have time for it and Simon thought it would be a great way to introduce you to how the high flyers party."*

"Party? Really? Where?"

"The annual IPC ball. It's on Saturday and Simon and Martin are going, along with their wives, of course, but we need a representative from the magazine itself. I would normally go but have zero time for frivolities and as you are stepping into my aching shoes, I thought you would enjoy it."

I feel excited as her words sink in. A ball. A real life ball! This is the stuff of fairy tales.

Sable says abruptly, *"I'll send the invitation over by courier. You have a plus one and the dress code is black tie and evening dresses. Oh, and Lily…"*

"Yes?"

I can't contain the excitement in my voice. *"You also need a mask. It's a masquerade ball which is irritating, but they operate a strict policy on the dress code, so you won't be admitted without one. Anyway, I must dash, lots to do and your holiday couldn't have come at a worse time, really. Never mind, it's my cross to bear, enjoy your time off while you have it."*

She cuts the call and I push away any guilt her words were designed to heap on me. No, I'm owed this time and it's her own fault she's leaving, not mine.

Mum looks interested. "Who was that dear, a gentleman friend perhaps?"

"No, of course not."

"What about that boy Kevin you're always going on about. Is he still in the picture?"

I feel embarrassed as I shake my head. "Um... no... Kevin and I, well, we're more friends than anything else."

I feel bad because I've used imaginary Kevin loads of times to get out of things I would rather not do. I really must stop acting like a child because Kevin has no room in my life when I become a high-flying, ball attending, editor-in-chief.

As I help mum clear away the remains of the roast dinner, we talk about the funeral arrangements.

"Things are moving fast, Lily. The invitations have gone out..."

"What invitations, it's not a party, it's a funeral?"

"Let me finish. No, they are tasteful black bordered white card, with silver inscriptions detailing the time and place of the funeral. We thought it best to deal with this in a professional manner as Aunt Daisy would have expected. We have also taken out an announcement in the Times, so I think every avenue is covered."

"Have you heard back from anyone?"

Mum looks angry. "Only that freeloader Elizabeth Watkins who now professes to be Aunt Daisy's best friend."

"Who is Elizabeth Watkins?"

"They went to school together, but quite honestly, I think they were only friends on Facebook because your dad can't remember her. Anyway, she got in touch, crying down the phone saying nothing would keep her away and could she possibly stay in Daisy's house as it's now empty because it would be what Daisy would have wanted. Oh, and also because she's currently having a cash-flow problem and can't really run to forking out for a hotel. She then had the cheek to fake cry and say that Daisy was always so generous in life and it would continue in death which is a memory she will always treasure."

I stare at her in shock. "You're not going to let her stay there – are you?"

"Of course not, I'm not stupid. I have been preparing for this and sent her a list of Air B&Bs in the area and told her there's a perfectly good hostel not far away either. I may have lied a little and said the house has been sealed off for evidence and is now under police guard. That seemed to do the trick and I haven't heard from her since."

Mum looks extremely pleased with herself and adds, "You know, it pays to be a quick thinker in times like this. Now, have you time for a brief run through of the service? Your father keeps on fluffing his lines which would spell disaster on the day."

Plastering a look of apology on my face, I say quickly, "I'm so sorry, mum, I've arranged to meet Heidi for a catch up. Maybe in the week, say Tuesday afternoon."

I know that Tuesdays are mum's body pump class and she lets nothing interfere with that, so she says somewhat irritably, "No, that won't do. Text me when you're free and I'll pencil in another date. You know, the sooner this organisational nightmare is over, the better I'll feel. Then again, it's the least I can do for poor Daisy, God rest her soul. I shouldn't complain, after all, she can't do it herself."

The tears spring to both our eyes and when dad wanders in from putting the bin out, he finds us sobbing in each other's arms.

He heads across and hugs us both, saying gently, "Let it all out, don't keep it in."

As we grieve for the woman who touched our lives so deeply, it makes me even more determined to make her proud and try to succeed where she failed. Maybe it's because I feel I owe it to her, or maybe it's because I'm recognising a lot of my own life in my Aunts and I would hate to have the same regrets looking back that she apparently did.

♥ 19

Heidi is already waiting when I dash into the Cuddle club around 8pm. Her face lights up when she sees me and she yells, "You made it and not a broken limb in sight. Well done my camping loving friend, come and tell me all the gory details."

Sliding into the booth beside her, I hug her warmly and am grateful for the pina colada she pushes my way. "Well, Heidi, it was definitely eventful, I'll say that for nothing."

As I fill her in, I love the way her eyes widen as each delicious detail leaves my lips. By the end of it, she is positively green with envy, which makes me feel amazing. Nobody is ever jealous of me because I do nothing but work but this has bucket list excitement written all over it.

At the end of my tale, she shakes her head. "Wow, that's some trip you just had. Do you think you'll ever see this man again?"

"Who Finn?"

Just saying his name makes me happy and without thinking, I glance at my phone and feel the disappointment hit me again when I see that he still hasn't called.

She looks thoughtful and says with interest, "So, what's next?"

"Meaning?"

"The list, what's your next move?"

"Well, I've been invited to a masked ball on Saturday night with the glitterati. That's impressive, isn't it?"

"With Finn?"

"Sadly no, in my new role as Editor in chief of Designer Homes - *on a budget*. I have to dress up and wear a mask and to say I'm excited is an understatement."

Heidi's eyes are wide as she says slowly, "Wow! It's just like Cinderella. Are you going ask Finn to escort you, I bet he would?"

The thought had already crossed my mind, but there is no way I could muster enough courage to ask, so I say happily, "Will you come? I'd really love to go there with you."

Heidi shrieks, causing a few eyes to turn our way and I laugh, "I'll take that as a yes."

She appears so excited she can't contain it and babbles on. "Oh my, I'll need a dress; a non-knitted one at that. Where will I find one and where's my fairy godmother when I need her? What are you wearing, Lily? We will have to compare outfit choices; do you even have an outfit; where will we find one and how are we getting there? Should I get my hair done and my nails, not to mention my bikini line? Should I learn ballroom dancing and do we get food before, during, or after?"

"Stop, it's too much." I shake my head laughing and watch Heidi take some deep breaths to try and contain her excitement.

"I thought we could hire our dresses from Prom Surprise in town. I'm sure they have a great selection, and I'm pretty sure I could find us a couple of matching masks on Amazon or the internet. We could get ready at my flat and call an Uber to take us there. You know, this is one tick on that list I'm going to enjoy."

"What's the tick?"

"A few actually. Dance under the stars with a man you've just kissed and buy something frivolous. I may take some ballroom dancing lessons before the big day, so that will be three ticks, thank you very much."

"Kiss a man, really, what will you do, just go up to a random stranger and plant one on him before pulling him onto the dancefloor? Goodness, Lily, you are so bold."

We giggle and she grins with excitement. "You know, I'm loving this list but you've forgotten one thing."

"Which is?"

"My compliment. I thought you were giving someone a compliment every day."

"Oh, I forgot about that. I did it one day, that should be enough. Actually, Heidi the list is a little bothersome if I'm honest. I'm so busy worrying about ticking the things off, I'm not enjoying them. You know, earlier I saw rain was forecast for Thursday and I'm already planning the song I'll sing when I grab my wellies and run out to sing in the rain. I've even thought of a good place for it that will look good in the selfie I intend on taking to record the memory. It's all becoming a little tedious and I wish I hadn't been so regimental in my approach to it."

"Then why don't you slack off a little? I mean, surely you should have your own list, anyway, and also, I thought these things were achieved in a lifetime, not a week. To be brutally frank, Lily, I think you're putting yourself under too much pressure on this. I fear that you'll burn out doing it and it will all have been for nothing. Maybe just ease off a little and let things take their natural course. Obviously, plan in some amazing trips and maybe take up a hobby but do what you want to, not what your Aunt wanted, I'm sure she wouldn't want it any other way."

I know she's right, but I feel as if I owe this to Aunt Daisy. Call it a parting gift to make her life more complete. I'm doing them in her memory and it's that thought that drives me.

Sipping my cocktail, I think about the task I've set myself. Maybe Finn was right, and what if I did everything on the list and was still unhappy? Would I make a new one and then another until I find what I'm looking for?

As our conversation turns to more usual things, I push away all thoughts of Finn and the bucket list and just enjoy a night out with my best friend. I'll work the rest out tomorrow because tonight I want to forget all the pain of the last week and focus on finishing a few more cocktails before I return home to plan my next move.

As it turns out, my next move was also one that earned me a tick off the list. Booking myself in for a taster lesson in Sylvia Robson's school of Ballroom dancing was inspired. I could certainly utilise the skills I will learn on Saturday night, and this place will tick the dance lessons box nicely. Sylvia is an impressive lady who apparently knew the sister of the woman who booked the backing singers for Strictly Come Dancing so she knows her stuff.

When I turn up, I feel a little apprehensive because knowing my luck everyone will be a professional dance champion or something. However, luckily, I appear to have joined the beginner's class because it soon becomes apparent that I know more than most of the people here, unless you count Clive and Rose who must be in their seventies and glide around the room like Frank Astaire and Ginger Rogers.

Connor, the man they partnered me with, is rather heavy footed and can't stop stamping on my feet every five minutes.

He appears extremely embarrassed at being partnered with me at all until I say as gently as I can, "Listen, Connor, why don't you let me lead for a bit? Nobody will notice and then if you get the hang of it, you can take over."

I smile and for the time the terror in his eyes subsides a little and he nods meekly. "Super, Lily. I'm sorry, I'm sure I'll get the hang of it soon."

Somehow, we manage to propel our way around the dance floor, or in this case the gym in the local comprehensive - out-of-school hours, of course. It brings back flashbacks of my own prom when I had the misfortune to be asked by Barry Gibbons, who was the most accident-prone pupil the school had ever seen. Half way through the theme to the Titanic, he spun me around and knocked Tracey Ironmonger into the stage, causing the portable light resting on it to fall off and shatter into a million pieces.

It went a little downhill after that when her date landed a huge punch on Barry who was not shy at reciprocating and they started a huge fight that practically destroyed all the hard work the prom committee had been slaving over for three months solid. Oh well, happy memories come back at the strangest times, reminding me why I gave up dancing – forever.

I am interested to discover more about my dancing friend and say with interest, "Why are you here, Connor?"

"I've got a date with a woman who loves to dance and I lied and said I could dance when I listed my interests and as she was the only one who replied to me, I have to learn and fast if I am to stand any chance with her at all."

"Maybe she lied too."

He shakes his head. "No, her profile picture on, The Love of Your Life, shows her holding up a glittering trophy."

"Well, it may be for something else, it may not be dancing at all, perhaps, I don't know, chess or something?"

He laughs while spinning me around a little too fast. "No, she was wearing one of those sequined dance dresses you see on the television. I think she's a professional."

"Oh, I see your predicament. Maybe you should come clean when you meet her. I'm sure it won't matter when she sees how amazing you are."

His face colours up and he appears a little stunned. "No one's ever called me amazing before."

He looks so happy it reminds me of the list where I vowed to compliment someone every day. Goodness, if I had known it would actually mean something to the person, I would have continued with it.

After two hours of intensive dance training, I feel as if I know enough not to embarrass myself on Saturday night if I'm lucky enough to be asked to dance. In fact, I'm quite looking forward to the whole experience and feel glad it's Heidi who will accompany me. In fact, life is certainly looking a lot more exciting than it did a few weeks ago, which reminds me that life can change in an instant. Once again, I feel sad when I think of how things changed for my Aunt, but I can't dwell on that. I need to remain positive and try to learn the lessons she has inadvertently taught me before I make the same ones because it's obvious, I was definitely heading the same way.

♥*20*

Heidi looks beyond excited and I share the same feeling. We are dressed like something out of a Disney movie. Two Disney Princesses off to the ball.

Heidi opted for a pale blue gown with a sequined bodice and tulle skirt that flows to the ground, tripping her up as she tries to work out how to walk on heels. Her brown hair has been curled and placed on top of her head with the back remaining long and flowing. She even found some pale blue satin evening gloves and a matching clutch and the fake diamonds she wears around her throat look positively magical. Her mask is an ingenious design of pale blue silk and rhinestones with a few ostrich feathers complimenting the outfit. She looks amazing and has an inner glow, and I have never seen her look as beautiful as she does now.

As I contemplate my own reflection, I am quite proud of how I brushed up for the occasion. My strawberry blonde hair is much the same as Heidi's but I have opted for the full 'up do.' My dress is a beautiful coral red satin, with a jewel-encrusted bodice. I too have some black evening gloves and matching clutch, and my mask is a mixture of black velvet and red feathers, with beautiful black jewels sparkling on the sides.

The doorbell rings and we grin at each other with anticipation. Heidi whispers, "This is it; we're going to the ball in our uber chariot. I can't cope."

Giggling like a couple of teenagers going to the school disco, we head downstairs and the taxi driver says gruffly, "Where to?"

"The Connaught rooms, Covent Garden."

He nods and ushers us to his waiting cab and jumps in, leaving us to open the door for ourselves. So much for the footmen. We appear to have the budget variety.

However, nothing can dull our excitement as we speed off into the night to an adventure we never knew was waiting. Heidi pinches herself and then me and says loudly, "I can't believe it. We're actually doing this. Do you think we'll meet someone?"

"I think that's a definite, after all, we're not going to be the only ones there."

"No, someone as in 'the one.' You know, as moments go, this one is the stuff of dreams. What if both our Prince Charming's are there and better still, are best friends? It would all work out rather well, wouldn't you say?"

"It would, but I doubt such things happen in real life. It will probably be the dullest thing we've ever had to endure because if it was that good, I'm pretty sure Sable would be sitting here in our place."

Heidi nods, looking a little crestfallen. "I suppose so."

By the time we reach the venue, we have imagined everything under the sun and have now both married Prince's from neighbouring countries by the end of our taxi ride.

As we pay the driver and step out onto the cobbled streets of London, we look in awe at the red carpet stretching out majestically from the entrance to the Connaught rooms.

Feeling extremely important, we make our way to the end of it, joining other partygoers who are also dressed to impress. Sable was right. The dress code is strict because I have never seen so many fine women and handsome gentlemen in my life. All are wearing masks which adds to the excitement and I nudge Heidi as we see an impressive looking man entering the venue just ahead of us.

Heidi gasps and says in a high-pitched voice, "Oh my, please say he's single and ready to mingle because I will die if he is isn't."

Her hand flies to her mouth and she says apologetically, "I'm sorry, I didn't mean..."

"It's fine, just a figure of speech, don't panic about it."

I smile reassuringly and we make our way inside and hand our invitations to the lady and gentlemen waiting on the door. The lady smiles and lets us pass and I feel as if I have socially arrived. I am now deemed respectable and allowed to party with high society, which proves to me that this job is the only thing that matters. If it opens up this new world of opportunity, I would be a fool to let it slip from my greedy, ambitious grasp.

An impressive staircase stretches out ahead, and I physically ache to glide up its steps to the promised land. I think we both hold our breath as we ascend the staircase and head toward the ballroom. As we step through the doors into a scene from a movie, I gasp with admiration. Heidi says in awe, "It's just like I dreamed it would be."

Huge chandeliers hang from the ceilings and all around is luxury on a rather large scale. The ballroom is certainly impressive and the dancing has begun already as handsome gentlemen spin their elegant companions around the floor.

We are approached by a waiter in a braided uniform, who offers us both a glass of what appears to be champagne. As we help ourselves, I congratulate myself on making it. I've arrived. I'm an important powerful lady.

We make our way through the crowds and I look for a familiar face behind the mask. I do know quite a few editors from other magazines and of course, the ones we are affiliated with. It doesn't take long before I spy Anastasia Martin, the Editor for Belle magazine, and I pull Heidi over to meet her. "Anastasia, it's me, Lily, from Designer Homes - *on a budget*."

She looks across and says pleasantly, "My dear, how amazing you look. Congratulations on the step up by the way. Sable told me you were her replacement."

As I bask in her praise, I remind myself that this woman used to ignore me whenever she breezed into our office to meet her friend for lunch. She was never interested in me, but that appears to have changed because she takes hold of my elbow and whispers, "My door is always open if you need a friendly ear to listen to your woes. Us girls need to stick together because we have to work twice as hard as the men to earn less. Sad fact but true, but hopefully times are changing. Sable and I shared many confidences and I hope we can do the same."

Reaching into her bag, she pulls out her business card and whispers, "My private number. Add it to your contacts and when you take over, ask your assistant to call mine and set up a lunch date. We have lots to discuss."

Without even acknowledging Heidi, she glides off and takes the hand of a rather distinguished gentlemen who guides her onto the dance floor.

"Who was that bitch?" Heidi whispers and I laugh out loud. "Bitch is the right description and to answer your question, no one important."

As I place the card in my bag, I vow not to call her for lunch. I still can't stand the woman and have no desire to confide anything to her.

As the evening progresses, we find a few people to talk to, but to be honest, it feels a little flat. This isn't panning out how I thought it would and aside from the odd familiar masked face, it's like being cast loose in a sea of strangers. I suppose half way through the evening, Heidi nudges me and whispers, "Don't look now but there's a man over there who's been staring at you all evening."

"Me?"

I make to turn and she hisses. "Not now. In a minute turn around as if looking for the waiter and clock the guy standing by the fire exit. Tall, dark and incredibly sexy with a black mask."

Feeling a little foolish, I do as she says and my eyes stare straight into the darkest eyes I have ever seen. Gleaming black hair, frames an incredibly handsome face, at least I think he's handsome because his mask obscures my view. As Heidi said, he is looking at me with such a lustful look I feel quite violated and turn quickly away. "Wow, you were right. I wonder who he is?"

Heidi shrugs. "I'm not sure but he appears to be on his own. At first, I thought he was looking at me but then realised, as usual, he wasn't. What will you do if he comes over?"

"I'm not sure. He looks a little intense."

Heidi nods. "You could say that. Sexy, though. He may be the stranger you need."

For some reason, my legs shake a little as I imagine being anywhere near the intense looking man and then we hear, "May I have the honour of dancing with the most beautiful girl in the room?"

Looking up, I see a good-looking young man, with sandy blond hair, wearing a rather fetching mask decorated with braid and feathers. He is smiling at Heidi who appears to have lost the power of speech, as she just nods and take the arm he offers her. Laughing to myself, I watch with interest as they take to the floor and his arm encircles her waist with a confidence that makes me smile. He then sweeps her off to dance and by the look on her face she is loving every minute of it.

Suddenly, I feel the gentlest breeze on the back of my neck and inhale a scent so intoxicating it brings my senses alive. Then a voice whispers in what appears to be an Italian accent. "May I have the pleasure of this dance, bella ragazza?"

My breath hitches because I know it's *him*. The dark disturbing man from the fire exit and as I turn, his arm wraps around me and he spins me so quickly I don't know which way we go. I am pulled tightly against a hard-masculine chest encased in a black tuxedo. I can't even raise my eyes to look at the man who has literally swept me off my feet, as we spin around the room like something out of Strictly. His hand gently caresses the small of my back and as I feel his fingers tease my naked skin, I shiver with something I never thought I had in me. Desire.

One dance becomes two and we still don't speak. He draws circles on my back and involuntarily I press closer against his hard body. He whispers strange words in my ear, and just the sound of them makes me weak with longing. This is the stuff of dreams. I wonder if this is what Aunt Daisy experienced? European love with a man who is so perfect he should be in a museum for women's fantasies.

On the third dance, he whispers, "Le cose belle arrivano quando non le cerchi."

"What does that mean?" I whisper, so turned on I can't cope.

His breath fans my face as he says huskily, "Beautiful things come when you're not looking."

I'm glad I'm wearing a mask because I must be as red as the dress I'm wearing. Luckily, I don't need to reply because suddenly, I am whisked through the doors onto a roof top terrace that sparkles with strings of fairy lights and flickering church candles.

The music is now fainter and yet still provides the tune for our dance, and as my partner guides me around the terrace, I feel my heart thumping with anticipation and every nerve inside me is standing to attention.

As we dance, he pulls me closer and strokes my cheek with a feather light touch and I almost cry as I see the stars twinkling in the black sky above. Leaning down, he whispers, "Sei Bellissima. You're beautiful."

Leaning back, I look into those dark eyes and my breath hitches as I see the stars twinkling above his head and watch his mouth lower to mine. As our lips meet, the moment feels intoxicating, forbidden and dangerous and as we share a long lingering kiss, I feel like a princess.

One kiss turns to two, then three, and when he pulls back, his eyes glitter in the darkness and I shiver at how intense they are. He says huskily, "You are cold."

Wrapping his arm around me, he spins me so my back is to him and folds me inside his jacket where the heat caresses my bare skin and makes me tingle inside. For a moment, we look out across the skyline and I swear I see a shooting star. Then he kisses the back of my exposed neck with soft, delicate kisses and I melt inside. I lean back against him and want this moment to last forever. As moments go, it's perfect – he's perfect and I can't believe my luck.

Then, almost as quickly as he came, he goes, moving away swiftly and as I turn, I just see his back disappearing through the double doors into the ballroom. Quickly, I hitch my skirt and follow him inside, but he has apparently drowned in a sea of people. Frantically, I look for him everywhere but quickly realise he doesn't want to be found.

As I touch my lips where his were last, my heart sinks as I realise, he's gone. Just for a second, I stand alone and confused, and then a feeling of excitement grips me as I realise what just happened. I danced under the stars with a man I just kissed, and that's all that matters. A one off, a brief interlude and a memory to cherish forever. The fact it was the most romantic moment of my life means I'll always remember it and one day I will look back on it and appreciate it for what it was. A moment in time so special nothing will ever tarnish it. It will always sparkle in my memory and never fade with the usual arrows that life aims at us.

As Heidi walks up, hand in hand with her own Prince Charming, I smile happily because from the look in her eyes, she has fared one better than me.

As they swap numbers and make plans to meet the next day, I am happy for her, knowing it's doubtful I will ever meet my stranger again. Then again, maybe I will, only the stars know the answer to that.

After the excitement of the ball, real life hits hard. Being on leave from work is great if there's something exciting to do, but the only thing occupying my mind at the moment is the list. I still haven't heard from Finn, which means he, like the Italian stranger, are just delicious moments to savour when I need them. I'm feeling quite low about everything, especially as Heidi appeared to grab all the luck that night and has started dating Thomas Everett, the man she danced with at the Ball. He works for a men's magazine and is responsible for a team of people who sell the advertising. He seems a great guy and I'm happy for them both but I still feel cheated out of something.

Mum looks at me sharply as I stir my tea relentlessly. "What's up?"

"Nothing."

"Yes, there is, you've stared into that cup of tea for five minutes and I can read your expression like a book."

"What does it say then?"

"That something's up."

Setting the teaspoon down, I sigh heavily. "I'm just unsure about things at the moment. I mean, Aunt Daisy's death has really shaken me up. I never thought she would die so suddenly and it's made me look at my own life a little more carefully."

"In what way?"

"Well, there are a lot of comparisons in our lives. We are both successful, although she was way more successful than me, but I still have time. Both of us have never met 'the one' and I'm worried that I'll end up the same as her, alone."

Mum's eyes soften and she reaches out and squeezes my hand.

"You're still young, Lily. Thirty may seem ancient to you, but really you're just starting out. Love will find you when you least expect it and the only thing you have to do is give it the opportunity."

"What do you mean?"

She smiles. "Get out more, join a club where young men go. Try internet dating but only reputable sites and never give your personal details out to anyone – mother's orders. Don't bury yourself in work all the time and look at the bigger picture. Just live life, darling, and don't become all work and no play because where's the fun in that? You see, you need to strike a balance between the two. It's all well and good having money and power, but what's it worth if you've got no one to come home to at night? You need someone to share your success with and your failures. Someone who will always have your back and be there when you need them the most. We are not designed to be solitary animals, darling, although God help me, I'm tempted sometimes."

We laugh and she smiles brightly. "Even though I moan constantly about your father, I wouldn't be without him. He's the salt to my pepper and the left shoe to my right one. We go together and one without the other is virtually useless. You need to find your pairing, darling, and then you will see that life is a lot more meaningful."

I know she's right, in fact, she says it most weeks anyway, but it's easier said than done.

"Easy for you to say, mum. For instance, I thought doing this list would open up a few opportunities. You know, like Aunt Daisy. I thought I might find that special someone as I believe she did once. The thing is, the men I've met so far are a little strange if you ask me."

"In what way?"

"Well, there was my camping trip leader, of course."

My heart leaps at just the mention of Finn's name and mum looks interested. "Tell me about him."

"There's not much to tell, really. He was rude, abrupt and condescending, but he grew on me. It was only two days, but I thought we reached an understanding but he hasn't even called once."

"Was he supposed to?"

"Well, not exactly but..."

"Why don't you call him then?"

"And say what?"

"I don't know, pretend you left something behind and did he find it? Say you're thinking about booking another trip and can he recommend one? You know, the list is endless with just a little imagination."

"No, if he wants to call me, he will. I'm not looking desperate. Anyway, then there was the man I danced with at the ball."

Mum looks interested. "Tell me more, in fact, that was over a week ago, why are you just telling me now?"

Ignoring her annoyed expression, I shrug. "Again, there's nothing to tell really. We danced a little and maybe shared a romantic kiss and then he left when my back was turned and I didn't even get to know his name."

"Typical Italian. Love them and leave them just as quickly."

Suddenly, she looks worried. "Oh my goodness, you don't think…"

"What?"

She leans closer and whispers, "That it was Aunt Daisy's Italian friend, the one who is now on the run."

I start to laugh and she says crossly, "Don't laugh, Lily, it could be more than just a coincidence for all you know. Maybe he tracked you down to the ball and targeted you. I've seen this happen many times before. He's a serial killer and is targeting rich and powerful women. He has disposed of Aunt Daisy for reasons only known to him, and now you're next in line. I'm guessing he knows everything about you. He's probably got one of those photographic walls in his apartment and is planning his next move. You're not safe."

"Who's not safe?"

My dad enters the room looking tired and my heart goes out to him. He has a lot on his plate at the moment with the funeral and his usual business, and it's definitely taking its toll.

Sinking down on a bar stool, he rips off his tie and says wearily, "I could murder a cup of tea, Sonia. Anyway, I repeat, who's not safe?"

Mum folds her arms. "Lily."

Dad looks alarmed and I shake my head. "Don't listen to her. I told her I danced with an Italian man at the ball and now she thinks he's Aunt Daisy's murderer coming after me. Honestly, mum. You really should get a hobby or something, you're getting worse."

Dad shakes his head and laughs softly. "She'll never change, she's always had an unhealthy interest in murder most foul. I blame the fact Midsomer murders is on most days clouding her mind."

Mum shrugs. "Well, I'm just saying."

She heads over to make the tea and I say softly, "Are you ok, dad?"

"Yes darling, I'm fine but I heard from the coroner today."

Mum looks up sharply and I see the excitement spark in her eyes. "Is it… murder?"

I think she holds her breath as dad rolls his eyes. "No, it's as I said, a heart attack brought on by several blocked arteries. Apparently, she didn't stand much of a chance and at least it was quick."

Mum almost looks disappointed. "So, we can go ahead with the funeral then."

He nods. "Yes, I think it's looking like the 13th so we should get in touch with her friends and family and finalise the arrangements."

We fall silent as we contemplate the upcoming funeral. This is it, the last thing we can do for Aunt Daisy and it seems so final. Once again, my thoughts turn to the list and I feel a renewed interest for the task.

Mum hands dad his tea and says with interest. "So, what else have you accomplished on that list of yours?"

"Not a lot really. I'm learning that most of the things require either a trip to the seaside or abroad somewhere. These are monumental things that you can't find in the high street, you know. Take riding an elephant. I'm not sure they allow that at London Zoo, if they even have any. Then there's to ride a horse on the beach. That requires a lot of planning, and I don't think it includes the donkeys on Bournemouth beach. You see, I'm learning that it's all well and good wanting to do these things but near impossible to do them in four weeks. I need to re-think this list because I can't see how it can be done."

I watch my parents share a knowing look which irritates me. "What's that look for?"

Mum smiles softly. "Put the list on hold for a while, darling. It will just tear you apart. Maybe now the funeral is going ahead we can get that out of the way and you can book a week away somewhere nice. Try not to think of the list and you'll probably find it just happens naturally, anyway. Chill out, darling and go with the flow, it's for the best, take my word for it."

Reluctantly, I have to admit that she makes sense for a change. The list is one thing, but it's lacking that special ingredient that makes it special. So far all it's brought me is trouble and heartache and I think she's right. I'm going to park it for a while and concentrate on *me* for a change.

♥*22*

Exactly ten days later, the morning of the funeral arrives and I can't believe it's here at last. We have gathered at mum and dads where the cars are arriving to take us to the church, and I think we're all relieved that the day has finally come.

The dress code is to wear bright colours because Aunt Daisy was always fond of dressing extrovertly. She hated black and banned it from consideration on any house she designed, and there was not a trace of it in her wardrobe.

I'm wearing a fuchsia pink satin dress and mum is pretty in canary yellow. Dad has his safari suit on and nan is wearing her red polka dot dress and pink shoes. Grandad is in navy blue with a green shirt and the only one missing is my brother Mark who couldn't make it back from Australia in time.

The doorbell rings and mum sighs. "Here we go."

She returns with dad's cousin Veronica and her husband Tony. True to the theme they are dressed accordingly and my aunt's dress is a pretty pale blue and uncle Tony looks splendid in his beige suit.

My aunt moves across with outstretched arms and hugs my nan crying, "You poor thing, I'm so sorry Auntie Sandra."

Nan's eyes fill with tears and my grandad wipes his own away. I feel so bad for them both. They

175

aren't in the best of health themselves, and this is devastating.

Luckily, the funeral director comes in and says reverently, "The cars are ready."

As we gather our things and make our way outside, my heart breaks as I see Aunt Daisy waiting for us in her coffin inside the white hearse. The flowers that cover her are bright and vivacious, and her name is spelled out in daisies of every colour.

As we stand and watch the car move slowly away, we steel ourselves for the ordeal ahead.

Several hours later and it's all over. We return home exhausted and emotional and yet with a feeling of closure.

As mum puts the kettle on, we sit around in the living room and nan kicks off her shoes and says sadly, "So, that's that then."

Grandad puts his arm around her and says softly, "We did her proud."

Nodding, nan gives a half smile. "She would have loved the service. You outdid yourself, David, your speech was so moving."

Dad just smiles sadly. "It was the least I could do. I still can't believe she's gone. She was always here and I never thought for one moment her life was going to be cut short."

Mum shouts from the kitchen, "David, I need a hand in here, if it's not too much trouble."

He rolls his eyes and heads off and I sit beside my nan who smiles sweetly. "You did well, treasure. It was a lovely speech you made; your aunt would have been proud."

My eyes fill with tears I thought had long since dried up and say in a small voice, "I'll miss her."

Mum heads into the room carrying the teapot and says loudly, "I see that Elizabeth Watkins came after all. Did you see what she was wearing?"

I look at her and shrug, "What was wrong with it?"

"It was black, Lily, black for goodness' sake, nobody wears black to a funeral, it's a disgrace."

"Actually, mum, they do, in fact, it's considered the norm, really."

She shakes her head crossly. "Not in this family they don't. Honestly, the disrespect shown after I made it my business to inform everyone of the dress code. Thank goodness she never stayed in Daisy's house, casting a shadow over it with her black dress. Daisy would turn in her grave."

I share a look with nan and her mouth twitches. Grandad rolls his eyes and I stifle a giggle.

Suddenly, the doorbell rings and we look at each other in surprise.

"Who can that be?" Mum jumps up and heads off to find out looking a little annoyed and nan says, "Who's that?"

"How do I know; I haven't got a sixth sense you know?" Grandad moans and then dad looks

177

concerned as mum says in a rather high voice, "Um… David, I think you should come out here."

We all look at each other in surprise as dad springs up from the sofa and rushes out to see who it is.

Straining to hear, we fall silent and hear muffled voices and then louder ones as they head our way.

As mum comes into the room, she raises her eyes and says awkwardly, "Um… this is a friend of Daisy's… Mr Bianci."

We look up in surprise as she is followed into the room by a very handsome man who looks to be around his late fifties. He nods and says with a deep Italian accent, "Please forgive me. My flight was delayed and I missed the service, I cannot apologise enough."

He looks at nan and grandad and his eyes fill with tears as he says hoarsely, "Your daughter was a Principessa. A goddess and the only woman I have ever given my whole heart to."

Nan looks completely shell-shocked and grandad looks confused. "I'm sorry, did you know Daisy?"

Holding out his hand, Mr Bianci shakes grandad's hand and says with tears in his eyes, "We were lovers."

We all stare at him in shock and he says with a break to his voice, "I am sorry, she never spoke of me, I know."

Mum looks unconvinced, but nan looks at him eagerly and pats the seat next to her. "Come and sit beside me…"

"Luca."

He smiles respectfully and she says softly, "Luca, come and tell us how you knew Daisy."

We all take our seats and look at the new arrival with interest as he starts to speak.

"We met in Sicily when Daisy was visiting a friend of my sisters."

Nan interrupts, "Ooh, I remember when she went there. It was to visit that woman whose house she re-modelled in Leatherhead."

Grandad still looks confused and dad says, "Let Luca speak."

We look at him expectantly. "Yes, Sophia was my sister's friend. She moved here for work and Daisy and her became good friends. When she returned home, they stayed in touch, which was how I met her."

"How old was she then, Bert? Can you remember?"

Grandad says with exasperation, "How do I know? I can't even remember my own age these days, let alone anyone else's."

Dad interrupts, "I think she must have been around thirty. I remember when she went to stay with her friend because she was full of it when she came home. I don't think she mentioned you though, Luca, I'm sorry."

I can see mum staring at him with suspicion and feel sorry for the poor man but he just nods and says sadly. "Because I was married at the time."

We all squirm a little and he shakes his head. "My wife and I were unhappy. We had rushed into marriage and were regretting it."

Mum rolls her eyes behind his back and nan looks a little annoyed, so I smile at him reassuringly as he carries on. "Daisy was beautiful inside and out. She would light up any room she entered, and her laughter made the sun come out. She was perfect and when she looked at me, everything else faded into the background."

He looks at my grandparents and says with some sincerity, "We started an affair that summer and it tore us apart. My wife was no longer interested in me, and Daisy was everything I had ever wanted. When she returned home, we decided it had to be the end, as painful as it was. Despite what you think, I am an honourable man and it was never an option that I would leave my marriage."

Nan looks at him with a bitter look and grandad says awkwardly, "Yes, probably for the best."

Luca says sadly, "Two years later my wife left me for another and my first thought was to contact Daisy again. She flew out to see me and it was still there. That bond we had that I knew was special. Once again, we spent time together with none of the restrictions of the past. I begged her to move to Italy to be with me, but she wouldn't. She told me her life was in London, where she had success. She couldn't leave that behind and live with me in a place she had no connections to."

"Sounds like Daisy." Nan seems rather annoyed and grandad nods in agreement. "That doesn't surprise me, she was always headstrong."

Mum appears to have thawed a little and says softly, "I'm so sorry, that must have hurt."

He nods. "It was the utmost pain a man can ever feel. To have found the greatest love, only for it to slip through his fingers, taking his heart with it."

Dad rolls his eyes, but none of us are interested. This is so beautiful. A tale of star-crossed lovers who never realised their passion. Wow, who knew?

Mum says, "Why couldn't you come to London and work here? Surely that would have solved your problem?"

"Sadly, it was never an option. I own several vineyards in Italy and my family relies on them. I am the head of the household and had to put my family and responsibilities first. We have produced wine for several generations and the vineyard is bigger than me. It has to come first."

Nan turns to grandad. "Ooh we love a nice drop of wine, don't we Bert?"

Luca smiles. "Then it will be my pleasure to arrange a delivery for you to sample."

They look pleased as dad says, "For goodness' sake, mum, the poor man is pouring his heart out and all you can think of is placing an order for his wine. Let the man finish."

Luca gives a half smile and say sadly. "Despite everything we kept in touch. Occasionally, we would meet up and take a holiday somewhere together. It became a long-distance romance, but Daisy always stopped herself from falling too hard. She told me she had loved once and that love had been taken from her without warning and she was scared to allow herself to have feelings again. She loved me but wasn't prepared to give everything up to be with me because she couldn't take the risk that it wouldn't work out, or something would happen to me."

Nan starts to cry softly and mum says in astonishment, "I never knew she was so scared of love. Poor Daisy, she missed out on so much out of fear."

Nan sobs. "She always was stubborn. She got that from her father."

Luca leans back and I'm mesmerised by the sudden change in his expression. It softens and the mask of grief he is wearing slips a little as he finishes his story. "Two weeks before she died, Daisy got in contact. She told me she had come to the decision to give our love a chance. She wanted to sell her business and move to Italy to be with me one hundred percent. I was to make the necessary arrangements and she would set things in place because she didn't want to ignore the love we both had. She was prepared to walk away from everything for love and that was when I think I was the happiest I had ever been. I told her I would fly out the same day and we could be together immediately, but she reassured me she needed the time to set things in place. She told me she had always loved me and was not prepared to put her life on hold any longer just for money and success. She wanted to live with me and experience love because she realised without love a person was the poorest they could be. When you called and told me of her death, the sun went out of my life and now all I have is bitterness and pain left. I will never find another Daisy and feel angry that we missed out on the greatest happiness two people can share. We wasted so many years that we could have been together and it is the cruellest conclusion to our story. I just wanted to come for one last time to meet the family of the woman I loved and tell you she meant everything to me."

There's silence as the tears fall freely once again, and we dwell on the pain this poor man must be going through.

Mum looks up and says gently, "Thank you, Luca, it was good of you to come all this way. Please, let me fetch you a drink and fix you some food, you must be starving. You must stay here tonight and we can talk some more, Daisy would have wanted that."

Dad and I look at her in surprise because suddenly Luca has gone from murderer to hero in thirty minutes flat.

He smiles gratefully and as mum heads to the kitchen, I follow her.

As soon as the door's closed, I whisper, "That poor man."

Mum nods. "It's a terrible story, yet the sweetest one at the same time. It's good to know Daisy met that special someone in life and experienced the feeling of the purest love. How sad though that it took her so long to realise its importance. Those poor people. What a life they could have had and she turned her back on it out of fear and success."

As she reaches for the kettle, she says softly, "It makes you realise what's really important in life, doesn't it, Lily?"

"Yes, it does bring it all into perspective."

As mum starts making Luca some sandwiches, I think about my own situation. If I find the man I love, I will not turn my back on him for success. At least Aunt Daisy's experience won't be for nothing. I will learn the lessons of the past and not make the same mistake. Now I just need to find that special someone and fast.

I've decided to go back to work early. After the funeral, I didn't feel much like having fun anyway, so decided to throw myself into my new job sooner rather than later.

It feels strange heading through the familiar doors as I have done for the past few years. Nothing has changed and yet everything has changed because for some reason, my heart isn't in it. Maybe it's because I've taken a break and the last few weeks have been so emotional.

As I make my way to my desk, I see Sable in her office shouting at somebody and I shiver inside. I know what it's like to be on the receiving end of one of her tirades, and I can only picture the poor person's misery as they take what she dishes out.

She notices me and gestures madly for me to join her and so, with a sinking feeling, I head towards her office.

As I open the door, she slams the phone on the desk and shouts, "How am I expected to navigate a sea of idiots?"

Her question, as usual, demands no answer, so I just smile sympathetically. However, as I look at her, I feel shocked because Sable appears to have aged overnight. Where poise and control usually sit well on her, it would appear they have deserted her now because she is looking frazzled, irritated and so tired she doesn't just have bags under her eyes, more like a whole baggage reclaim belt. She is pale and her face is pinched and her hair is in need of a hairdresser as a matter of urgency. Even her make-up looks rushed and her clothes are not as sharp as they usually are.

She sinks down wearily in her seat and sighs heavily.

"I'm struggling, Lily. Yes, I know it's hard to believe but life is severely testing me right now and I'm at my wits end."

I'm not sure what to say and just smile sympathetically and let her speak.

"Joseph Maltravers has called in sick which seriously raises doubts about him as your replacement."

Joseph Maltravers! I feel my blood boil as I think of the sneaky little slime bag getting his hands on my position. Joseph has worked in another division, doing much the same job as me, although concentrating mainly on advertising revenue. He's always looking to outdo me at every challenge we are set and I know he outsources most of his own work to others and passes the results off as his own. He has made no secret of his desire to step in my shoes because he believes he is above selling advertising space and wants to be more creative with his talent, as he is so fond of telling anyone who will listen.

However, now is not the time to vent my dissatisfaction at my replacement because as sure as

I'm going to be editor-in-chief, Joseph Maltravers will *not* be my deputy.

Sable sighs wearily and drums her fingernails on the desk. "I'm struggling, Lily."

She looks at me with a grave expression as I stare at her in shock. "Yes, I know it's hard to believe, but I have discovered a weakness I never saw coming."

She smiles wryly. "I can't be in two places at once."

She holds her hand up as if I would dare to interrupt and looks at me sharply. "I understand you still have two weeks left of your leave entitlement and yet have decided to return to work, which brings me to the conclusion you have run out of ideas on how to spend your time."

I make to speak, but she silences me with a look and smiles thinly. "You would be doing me a huge favour if you could take on one of my responsibilities yourself."

Suddenly, I feel the power washing over me. Me, taking on one of Sable's roles because she can't appear to cope. How the worm has turned.

Nodding enthusiastically, I speak for the first time. "Of course, I would be happy to help."

I wonder what it is. Maybe it's heading up the main feature of the month. I would love to organise that. Maybe it's restructuring the office. I can think of several changes I would make before lunchtime.

She reaches into her desk drawer and slides a business card towards me.

"I need you to go to the Château and supervise the deliveries."

As I stare at her in shock, she holds her hand up once again and smiles. "Don't thank me, I know it's a generous offer but my time is so valuable, I can't possibly be there to organise the renovation myself."

"But…"

"No buts, Lily, I have faith in your abilities, even if you don't. I have booked you on a flight from Gatwick this afternoon and a car will be waiting to take you directly to the Château."

She tosses a bunch of keys across the desk and says briskly, "Take the keys and the address is on the card. You will stay in the gîte located by the lake and supervise the deliveries, which are all detailed on the spreadsheet I have emailed to your inbox. Work begins on Monday so I will need you on hand as my eyes and ears. Any problems, call me but remember I am very busy and will rely on your judgement."

She stands signifying the end of the conversation and I say nervously, "But I don't speak French, how will I communicate with them?"

"You don't need to. I have arranged for an interpreter who will also be on hand during your entire stay. Don't thank me, Lily, because I know how important rest and recuperation are. Your aunt has died, leaving you stricken with grief. You are floundering, I can see that, and this is my way of getting your head back in the game. Ease in gently with a change of scenery and a slower pace of life. Two weeks should be enough time to recharge those batteries, leaving you fighting fit for the challenges ahead. Now, I am needed at the monthly meeting upstairs, so you will have to thank me another time."

She points to the door and I nod and meekly head through it. France! What on earth just happened?

Seven hours later and I feel every bump in the road as I bounce around in the back of the car that Sable arranged to meet me at the airport. The driver apparently speaks no English, either that, or he can't be bothered to talk and I am left staring out at the idyllic landscape as we speed through the streets of France towards the unknown.

The weather isn't very welcoming and the rain hits the car windows, providing a backdrop of misery to a landscape that looks as unwelcoming as the driver. I shiver as I feel the cool air of a heater that appears to be stuck on aircon and I shrink further into my jacket as I wish for the hundredth time that I was a stronger person and told Sable exactly what to do with her kind offer.

The car finally turns off the main road onto a road that has obviously seen better days. I look with interest at the trees that line the route as we pass through a rather large gate with an old sign hanging from the post.

Château de rêves. My heart sinks as I imagine the Château much like this sign. Old and decrepit and on its last legs.

As we pull up slowly into an old courtyard, my heart sinks further. Old cobblestones with weeds sprouting from the cracks look slippery and rather dangerous. The old stone of the Château looks in serious need of repointing, and the windows decayed and in need of repair and a good painter and decorator. Any plants that used to grow have been murdered by the ivy that is waging a war on the ancient building, and it appears that victory is not far away as it covers most of the front of the crumbling piece of French history.

However, even I can't take away the sheer romance of the place. The majestic towers that sit on four corners of the ancient building give it a delicious sense of romance and the view is a subject that any artist would die to recreate on canvas. The dramatic landscape that could be the setting of any Jane Austen novel calls to my soul and the nooks and crannies crying out to be explored are promising excitement and mystery for those who dare.

As I exit the car, I feel the spirit of adventure grip me as I see the sprawling grounds of a place that has not been loved for some time. I spy what must once have been an impressive landscaped garden and evidence that this place was once full of grandeur. There is history here that needs to be revisited and understood, and despite the trepidation

I felt on arrival, something about this place settles
my heart and it almost feels as if I'm home.

♥*24*

The driver hauls my case from the boot of the car and nods before returning the way he came, leaving me alone in a strange place feeling strangely at ease with myself.

Grabbing my case, I begin to wheel it towards the door, reminding me of when I last wheeled a case and I laugh to myself at how strange January is turning out to be. Two holidays in one month and a funeral. Aunt Daisy would be proud of my spirit of adventure.

Taking the large bundle of keys from my handbag, I struggle to find the right one. After the fifth attempt, the key turns in the ancient lock and the door creaks open under my gloved hand.

The air is slightly musty and there are cobwebs welcoming me in. It smells of ancient dust and stale air, and I shiver as I see the extent of the task ahead of Sable and Arthur. Fleetingly, I wonder if demolition would be a much better option, but as I look around at the crumbling walls and architraves; I see beyond the aged imperfections and discover the true beauty of the past.

Wooden floors creak underfoot as I move from room to room. It surprises me that I have no fear because anyone could be lying in wait for me, but it's as if I know I'm safe here. The building has a warm atmosphere which is the only warm thing about it and I smile with pleasure as I see the potential of a place that could be so amazing in the future.

As I explore, I see the sheer size of the task ahead. I count seven bedrooms and three bathrooms upstairs, some of which are accessed by small meandering staircases into the four turrets. I gasp at the views these rooms offer despite the grey vista outside and can only imagine the perfection they frame as the seasons change.

Downstairs was a large kitchen with only a rusting range cooker and long scrubbed wooden table left in residence. The large reception rooms were missing floorboards and the plaster was crumbling from the walls, but they all offered large ornate fireplaces that would bring any room to life when lit.

However, it is upstairs that brings me the most pleasure and it's solely because of the view. I could sit for hours on any of the small window seats, set in an alcove overlooking the lake, the orchard, or the wild gardens that have seen better days.

As I dream about the future and what this place will bring, I hear a door slam downstairs, which immediately makes me nervous. Someone's here.

My heart starts racing as I wonder who it could be. I'm not expecting anyone and maybe it's an intruder chancing their luck, or one of mum's murderers that appear to be freely on the loose just about anywhere.

Edging towards the door, I listen for voices and hearing none, swallow hard. Maybe I should just hide out in a cupboard or something until they get bored and leave. I'm not sure I'm ready to face anyone, and yet I am the keyholder and it's why I'm here after all. To oversee everything, so grabbing any courage I may have, I venture tentatively downstairs.

"Hello, are you here, Lily?"

A loud voice booms through the Château and I listen in surprise. That voice sounds rather familiar, but it can't be, I'm hearing things.

As I reach the bottom step, a man comes striding into the hallway and I almost rub my eyes in disbelief – Finn!

He turns and smiles as he sees me staring at him in shock. "We meet again, Adams."

"But how, what's going on, why are you here?"

Then I say in a whisper, "Are you following me?"

He throws his head back and laughs loudly, and I feel a little annoyed at his reaction. "Maybe I am, nothing gets past you, hey, darlin'."

"Explain yourself then because if you are following me, I want to know why?"

He grins and leans back against the ancient wood panelling and looks me up and down.

"Hmm, still overdressed as usual with completely the wrong clothing."

I stare down at my velvet leggings and UGG boots and feel annoyed. Ok, I admit a faux fur jacket is a little ostentatious for rural France and possibly the matching fur hat is a step too far but nobody will convince me that the adorable cream muffler doesn't finish the outfit off perfectly. So, I glare at him and say tightly, "Says the man who thinks standard army issue clothing is bang on trend. What's the matter, Finn, did you suffer a style bypass in your youth because you could certainly use some lessons?"

His eyes flash and he shifts from the wall and heads purposefully towards me, with a steely glint in his eye. Despite my bravado, I begin to shake inside because there is something so potent about the alpha male that appears to exist to taunt me every chance he gets. As he draws near, he leans down and whispers, "I missed you, Lily."

Well, I didn't expect that and just stare at him in shock. Then he reaches out and pulls me close and says softly, "Are you ready to strike a few wishes off your bucket list."

"What do you mean?" My voice is shaky and weak, completely against how I want to appear, and he strokes the side of my face and says softly, "This is the perfect opportunity to live dangerously. Make some memories to keep you warm at night. Throw caution to the wind and live on the edge. What do you say, Lily, will you let me show you how amazing life can be?"

For a moment, I think he's going to kiss me and I am so ready for it but then he pulls back and winks, "You know, I haven't been able to stop thinking about you and that list since you left. It made me question my own life and what I wanted out of it."

"Really."

Now I'm interested and he nods. "Yes, it made me question everything and the only thing that seemed to matter was that I saw you again. Why do you think that is, Lily?"

I almost can't speak but manage to say in a rather high voice, "I'm sure I don't know."

He looks thoughtful and then shrugs. "Well, maybe this is our chance to find out together."

Collecting myself, I say firmly, "Well, this is all a little strange if you ask me. I'm not sure I understand what on earth is happening here, but all I know is that I'm here to do a job and I'm not sure if Sable would be happy if I let somebody else stay here with me. I mean, the interpreter is due at any time, so it may be a little awkward. Maybe you should look for an air B&B in the meantime, or then again, you could always pop up your tent in the grounds, if you still have it."

I take a few deep calming breaths and try to get my head straight. Finn just throws me a cocky look and says, "Je suis ton interprète."

"What did you say?"

"I am your interpreter."

"But how, what's going on, seriously, are you stalking me?"

He grins and his eyes flash as he nods. "Yes, I am."

Taking a step back, I feel a little faint. "You are."

"Yes, you see, Lily, I engineered this whole invitation because I thought you may need someone to guide you safely through the list. When you told me you worked for the magazine, it was the gift that kept on giving."

"What do you mean?"

He laughs and says lightly, "Relax, I'm not a weirdo or anything."

"I'll be the judge of that."

He smiles gently. "Listen, I'm sorry but you see Arthur is my cousin and when you told me you worked with Sable, it was too good a coincidence to ignore. I engineered the whole mini break just so I could see you again and maybe help you with your list."

"But why? It's a bit extreme, isn't it?"

"I'm an extreme kind of guy. I thought it would be more of a memory this way. You could look back and see the romance of the situation and who knows, you may even enjoy my company. I had a few weeks to kill and as I'm fluent in French, along with a few other languages, I offered to help. Arthur and Sable were too busy to be here, and I thought of you. I mean, we never really got the chance to get know one another, so this is our chance."

I feel a little light-headed and say weakly, "Sable knew."

He nods. "Yes, when I told her I wanted to surprise you, she told me to leave it in her capable hands. I knew I could count on her because Sable is the type of woman who doesn't take no for an answer. Quite domineering in a lot of ways, but she gets results."

My head is spinning with the whole situation and Finn smiles. "Come on, I'll show you to the guesthouse. It's a lot more comfortable than this crumbling ruin and I'll make you a coffee and you can get warm by the fire and adjust to the situation."

Reaching out, he takes my hand and squeezes it gently. "It's ok, Lily, don't be worried. I can assure you I'm an officer and a gentleman and you are perfectly safe with me."

He leads me outside and I watch as he carefully locks up behind us before hoisting my case up with ease and saying lightly. "It's not far, just through those trees."

As I follow him down the cobbled path, I feel a growing sense of excitement. Finn is here - with me – for two whole weeks. Now the shock has worn off, I feel excited because from the look in his eyes, this trip is going to be one I will never forget.

♥25

As Finn said, the guest house isn't far and I'm interested to look inside the rather boring looking stone building with wood-smoke pouring from the chimney. Gingham curtains flutter at the windows, and the paint peeling from the large front door doesn't fill me with a lot of hope on the interior.

However, inside is perfectly charming. Although not my usual taste, I find a certain delight in the French antiquities that decorate the space. Wirework and pottery sit side by side on ornate dressers set behind comfortable armchairs. A riot of colour explodes inside the cottage, all battling for attention with each other because there is apparently no theme running through this room at all.

The warmth of the fire beckons me and as Finn sets my case down onto the flagstone floor, he says cheerfully, "Take a seat by the fire and get warm. I've made a pot of coffee and I have some soup heating on the range with some crusty bread. You must be starving after your journey, so you as may as well make yourself at home and let me run around after you for the next hour."

He heads off and I sink into one of the old velvet chairs by the fire and try to organise my mind. This is the strangest experience of my life, so far anyway, and yet I'm not afraid. Mum would imagine Finn to be some mad weirdo stalker with murder on his mind. However, I just have an increasingly warm feeling inside as I think about the lengths he has taken to spend time with me. Here I was thinking he wasn't interested and all the time he was planning this.

As my feet begin to thaw in front of the open fire, so do any reservations I may have had. He's right, this is a golden opportunity and maybe this will be my Aunt Daisy moment when she met Luca. Suddenly, it strikes me that maybe Finn is also married and as he heads back into the room carrying a large tray of goodies, I say quickly, "Just a quick question, Finn."

He looks at me expectantly as he sets the tray down on the wooden table before us. "Um, you don't happen to be married by any chance, do you?"

I think I hold my breath as I wait for his answer and he says incredulously, "Of course not, why?"

The relief makes me lean back in my seat and I laugh softly, "Just checking."

Handing me a bowl of soup, he says with interest, "Are you?"

"What?"

"Married?"

I say incredulously, "Of course not."

Grinning, he sits beside me and laughs softly, "Just checking."

Rolling my eyes, I eat up and I must say I'm feeling quite good about life right now. I have two weeks of excitement to look forward to with possibly the man of my dreams and no worries because as he can speak French, he can deal with the builders and deliveries.

After a while, I say thoughtfully, "You know, while I'm here, I may take up a new hobby."

"Like what?"

"Art."

He shakes his head. "I thought you'd already done that."

"No, this time I'll paint landscapes. I'm sure there must be an easel around here somewhere and a canvas. We are in France after all, the home of creativity and many famous painters."

"Maybe. Have you ever painted before?"

"No, but I'm guessing it's easy."

Finn laughs and throws another log on the fire. "So, what's happened, you've been here for at least an hour and I haven't seen you take a selfie once yet, are you feeling ok?"

"Of course, I'm just waiting for the right shot to reveal itself."

As I look around, it strikes me that this place could use a bit of a design makeover and say critically, "I can see what Sable meant. This place is a project. I wonder if she's secured the television series yet?"

Finn snorts. "In her dreams."

"Why not, as you said before, she's very domineering and gets results?"

"Because it's been done already. No, she'll be lucky to see any profit from this place inside of five years if you ask me."

"Why?"

"Because it needs a complete overhaul on the buildings alone before you can even start on the interior. The grounds need landscaping, and that's not cheap when you're talking on this scale. Then she will need to kit it out to appeal to the luxury market, and even with your skills on designing homes on a budget, it will still cost a small fortune. No, if you ask me, she'll get bored long before it's finished and either sell up, or delegate the job to staff."

He laughs. "If I know my cousin, he'll be the same. They like their creature comforts too much to suffer in poverty for long. As soon as the going gets tough, they'll be booking a trip to an all-inclusive paradise and turning their backs on this whole project."

"What makes you so sure?"

"Because I know them and they think everything can be bought and when they're paying they expect quick results. This place is a lifetime's work and they won't have the patience for that."

The flames from the fire illuminate Finn's face, and I find myself staring at him in wonder. I always knew he was handsome but here, inside this retreat with only each other for company, he seems a lot more relaxed than he did on the camping trip. He has softened a little and although he is still the best looking man I have ever spent time with, there's a lot that intrigues me about his life past the obvious attraction.

He hands me a coffee and I decide to delve a little deeper.

"So, what do you do for a living, Finn? So far I know you are good outdoors and appear to speak three languages."

"Five actually."

"Wow, what are the other ones?"

"Well, obviously English, although some say that's my weakest one."

He grins and I roll my eyes. "Then there's German and French, of course. I also speak Spanish and Italian."

Wow, I'm impressed and interested to hear why. "So, how did you learn them all? Did you do a course at evening college?"

He laughs and sits back in his chair and fixes me with a strangely intense look. "No, I needed to learn for my job. I spent some time in each country and picked up the language. Walter and Ryker helped me when I worked in Germany. I returned the favour with their English."

"You're right then."

"About what?"

"You are rubbish at English. They could hardly speak a word."

Finn laughs and shakes his head. "They're fluent, they are just very private people. They don't say a lot for a reason."

"Which is?"

"Because then they would have to answer questions they would rather not."

Now I'm intrigued and lean forward. "Tell me more."

Finn looks a little worried and shakes his head. "I'm sorry, Lily. I can't speak about them, or the job we do. It's probably best you don't ask. Maybe I'll tell you more when I know you better."

He looks away as I stare at him in surprise. Why won't he say? An uneasy feeling creeps through my body and I say slightly nervously, "It's not illegal is it?"

For a moment he doesn't answer and looks a little uncomfortable. "Not exactly but it's not nice, so it's best you forget about it."

Standing up, he gathers the tray and says cheerfully, "Ok, I'll wash and you can dry, then I'll show you to your room. Tomorrow we begin the adventure, but tonight you will probably just want to grab some sleep. You must be tired after that journey and I have some things I need to do."

He doesn't look at me as he heads off to the kitchen, leaving me feeling a little unsettled. What is it he does and why won't he say? He looked so uncomfortable when I asked, and it's only made me more determined to find out.

As I follow him, I'm starting to think this is the strangest day of my life and yet something is telling me it will be all be ok, at least the fool in me is saying that. The sensible part of me is shrieking at me to get out of here as soon as possible because nothing is adding up. Too many coincidences and a lot of unanswered questions. Maybe I should never have come, but for the first time in my whole thirty years, I feel alive.

The room he showed me to is basic in the extreme. Bare wooden floors with just a thin cotton rug. A big brass double bed with covers that look as if they've never seen a washing machine. Even the pillows look old and have lost their stuffing and the lack of ensuite facilities is all too obvious as I spy a water pitcher and bowl standing on the wooden chest that my nan wouldn't be seen dead owning. The curtains at the window are a little jaded and don't appear to act as any deterrent to the light outside. Even the old Armoire in the room looks to be the entrance to Narnia and I shiver as I face the prospect of staying here for two weeks.

Finn leaves me to it and I wonder what he does.

However, my phone rings interrupting my thoughts and I'm happy to hear Heidi on the other end.

"Lily, where are you? You mum said something about going to France."

"She's right. Sable asked me to oversee some work at her new Château but before you get excited, this place is a dump."

I feel a little bad about my description because actually, I love the quirky little place but Heidi is a dreamer and would have been imagining some sort of fairy palace, so I needed to set her straight about that before I start posting artistic shots on Instagram.

"Anyway, what's up, why are you calling?"

I detect the excitement in her voice as she squeals, *"Thomas and I are going to the Maldives on an all-inclusive week away. He won it in the raffle at work and asked me. Can you believe my luck?"*

Looking around me, I imagine her five-star luxury compared to my two star one and feel a little jealous if I'm honest.
"Great, when do you go?"

"Monday. It's so exciting. The thing is, I was hoping you'd cover for me at Nouveau Knitting. I knew you were off and thought it worked out perfectly."

I know it's wrong of me but I feel relieved because the thought of running her crazy business is not my idea of fun.
"I'm so sorry, babe, you can see I'm out of the country."

She groans. *"Never mind, I'll ask my mum instead. She's itching to get her hands on my business, so I'm sure she'll leap at the chance."*

I feel bad because Heidi's mum is a nightmare. By the time she comes home, I expect her shop will be re-organised, probably re-decorated and a whole load of new classes added to the working day. She will have arranged supplier visits and bought everything she thinks is a good idea, which in reality is useless and probably bankrupt Heidi in the process. I feel like the worst friend in the world and say apologetically, "I'm sorry. Is there anyone else? I mean, it may be safer to close for the week."

"Maybe, it's a possibility. Anyway, tell me about your trip, what's that all about?"

Excitedly, I fill her in and she shrieks loudly, *"That's so romantic. You are so lucky. You know, this is the stuff of dreams and you must keep me updated on how things go. I mean, do you think you'll... you know?"*

"What?"

"Do that thing on your list?"

"What thing?"

"Have sex with a stranger on the beach."

"No, I won't and do you know why?"

"Why?"

"Because that item has already been ticked off and it's January for goodness' sake. I'm struggling to take my coat off, let alone the rest of my clothes. In fact, it's looking doubtful that I'll even change for bed because this room I'm in apparently has no heating and the only way these clothes are leaving my body is if there's some form of heat keeping the cold out."

"I'll bet Finn has some heat he can throw your way."

Heidi giggles and I say crossly, "There will be none of that, no, this trip is a learning experience of a different kind."

She laughs, and I know that I'm only fooling myself. Seeing Finn again reminded me of how sexy he is. Even I know that at the first opportunity, I'm ditching my principles in a jiffy, just for one stolen forbidden moment with him.

Heidi interrupts my thoughts and says gently, *"Well, I should call my mother. Keep in touch though and don't spare any of the gory details. I'll keep you informed on my own love trip and we can compare notes."*

We say our goodbyes and as she cuts the call, I'm happy for her. At least one of us gets the exotic holiday.

As I settle down for the night, I change into my onesie under what passes as a duvet and hope that the bed is warm because this trip is not the luxury one I hoped for. Thinking of Finn in the nearby room is fuelling my fantasies, and he invades my dreams as I sleep.

When I wake the next morning, it's to the sound of activity and what appears to be some kind of lorry reversing outside my window.

Quickly, I grab my phone and see that it's 10am already and groaning, I leap out of bed and shiver as an icy blast hits me. Grumbling to myself and imagining all sorts of revenge on Sable at my hands, I struggle into the warmest clothes I brought with me and head outside to see what all the commotion is.

The courtyard is a hive of industry and I see several lorries and vans congregating outside the Château and in the middle of it is Finn, directing them where to go and shouting in what I assume is French.

Just for a moment, I savour the sight of him. He is so commanding, so rugged and so manly, that I feel instantly heated by my own thoughts. If anything, my memory of him didn't do him justice because he appears larger, more muscular and more dominating than I first thought, and as his eyes meet mine across the courtyard, I see the interest reflected right back at me.

Just for a moment, we lock looks and the rest of the world fades away. I almost catch my breath because this moment promises so much and I will be so disappointed if it doesn't deliver what it says on the tin because from the look in Finn's eyes, my stay here is going to be the stuff of dreams. It's only when I hear a yell, that I look away and see a man gesticulating wildly as a lorry tries to reverse in my general direction.

Jumping out the way, I watch as the builders offload their cargo and I can see that Sable has been very busy with her shopping list.

What was once a ramshackle courtyard in the land that time forgot, is now transformed into a builder's yard. All around me the men organise themselves and I can only watch in fascination.

After a while, Finn wanders over and smiles. "Morning, Adams. Did you sleep well?"

"As well as can be expected."

Finn breaks off and shouts something in French and then turns back and smiles.

"I don't suppose you could fix them some coffee? They appear to run better on it and we may get some progress by the end of the day."

"Of course, leave it with me."

Quickly, I head back to the guest cottage and try to unscramble my mind. Being here with Finn is amazing, but we do have a job to do after all and the builders will need a steady stream of encouragement if this place is ever going to take shape.

For most of the day, we settle into our roles. Finn liaises with the builders and I keep them all fed and watered. I am surprised to see what appears to be a delivery of French bread and cheese with some ham and olives in a wicker basket on the kitchen table. As I prepare the meal, I savour the simplicity of the

French way of life which is so different from my one in London.

I find the day goes quickly and by the time the last builder leaves, I feel strangely happy and satisfied on a day well spent. They were all so appreciative of the simplest thing, like a coffee and a reviving biscuit to keep them going. Finn dipped in and out and I enjoyed working alongside him, happy at the cheeky winks he gave me and the sexy smile that made my soul heat up.

As soon as the last builder leaves, calm is restored and Finn groans. "That was full on. I don't know about you, but the last thing I want to do is cook this evening. How about we find a nice little restaurant in the nearest town and treat ourselves to some French cuisine?"

"That sounds like the best idea you've had since I met you."

We share a smile and it makes me happier than I thought it would.

By the time we get washed and changed, the light is turning to dusk and Finn smiles. "You did well today."

"What, make a few coffees and some food, it was hardly rocket science."

"No, but it was demanding. Not much of a holiday for you."

"It's fine, holidays are overrated, anyway."

We head out in Finn's car and I quickly turn the heater on full blast. "You know, Finn, it says something when the car is warmer than the cottage. I may just sleep in here tonight."

"Why, were you cold last night?"

"Freezing. They obviously forgot to put central heating in my room. I was warmer when we were camping."

Finn looks a little upset and says apologetically. "I'm sorry, Lily. I forgot about the heating. I had a fire in my room and thought you had too. Maybe you should have my room tonight, I'm used to extreme conditions."

I hold my breath because any sliver of information about Finn and his life interests me way more than it should and I say nonchalantly, "So, you spend a lot of time outdoors."

"Yes, you could say that."

"Does it involve camping?"

"Sometimes, sometimes not."

I feel a little exasperated and say impatiently, "You may as well tell me what you do, Finn because if you don't, I'll ask Sable."

"You can if you want, she doesn't know either."

I stare at him in surprise and he says flatly, "It's not something I talk about and I'm not prepared to start now. Just know it's nothing to worry about."

We fall silent and the curiosity is burning me up inside. Finn is an enigma. On the one hand, he's open and chatty and yet he has this mysterious side to him that fascinates and intrigues me.

As we park outside a bistro, I joke, "Then I will just have to get you drunk so you tell me everything in a drunken stupor."

"You can try but I don't drink to excess. I never have and probably never will. You see, Lily, I know my limitations and have enough self-control to stop. I'm guessing you don't, so if we have a drinking contest, I'm guessing the only one spilling her secrets will be you. So, tell me now, do you have any secrets you want to tell me about, Lily?"

He stares at me with a deep, penetrating look and I feel myself flush as I feel guilty about things I haven't even done. Finn seems to be good at setting me on edge. It's like when I walk through the customs 'nothing to declare' channel in the airport. Even though I have nothing to declare as the name suggests, I walk with guilt written all over my face because I'm sure they are waiting to spirit me off to one of those sterile rooms to search me. I am always the one who can't keep a secret because just one sharp look is enough for me to spill everything from my lips and this is no exception because I say quickly, "I kissed a stranger at a masked ball."

♥27

Finn looks slightly stunned as I say quickly, "I mean, not that it's wrong or anything, it's just that, well, you know, caught up in the moment and all that."

Finn shakes his head and laughs incredulously. "Why is that a secret?"

Feeling a little foolish, I say quickly, "Well, obviously it's not, I mean, I'm a free agent and can do anything I want to. The thing is, I suppose, I'm, um, just not usually that kind of girl. I mean, I don't make it a habit to go around kissing sexy foreigners but it was kind of in the moment."

"What, like sleeping with your expedition leader?"

I stare at him in shock and he starts to laugh. "You know why I slept with you and it wasn't like that."

"Like what?"

"You know, naughty."

He starts laughing harder. "Naughty. You're priceless."

"And you're an asshole but we already established that."

I start to feel angry and it's not directed at Finn for a change. I'm angry with myself because why am I such an idiot? It's no business of Finn's if I *slept* with the masked man but for some reason it felt as if I had been disloyal to him but I don't know why.

Feeling embarrassed more than anything, I make to leave the car and to my surprise an arm pulls me back and he says softly, "Le cose belle arrivano quando non le cerchi."

Spinning around, I stare at him in total shock and he winks. "I didn't want you to experience your list with anyone but me, so I kind of intervened."

"You! It can't have been. He was nothing like you, don't tell me you paid someone to do it, an escort, or something."

He smiles gently. "No, it was me. When Felicity passed me the list, I committed it to memory. I spoke to Sable and she told me about the masked ball and I saw my opportunity to give you a memory to treasure."

"You did that – for me?" I gasp in astonishment and he nods. "Sable gave you two tickets to the ball and a third one for me. I was relying on you not taking a date, although it wouldn't have stopped me."

I stare at him in astonishment, as he says softly, "It was easy. I disguised myself by wearing a wig and different colour contacts, and with the mask it totally transformed me. I chose to be Italian because that sounds the most romantic when spoken. I watched you all night and then seized my moment when your friend was distracted."

I feel uneasy. "That was genuine, wasn't it? I mean, Thomas isn't part of this – is he?"

"Relax, I wouldn't know the guy if I saw him again. No, this was all about giving you a memory to cherish forever and me a little excitement at the same time. You see, Lily, like I said, your bucket list got me thinking and the more I thought about it, the more I wanted to be the one to do those things with you. Thinking of you out there looking for experiences worried me and if I'm honest, made me jealous."

"Jealous, but why, you hardly know me?"

Taking my hands in his, he gazes deep in my eyes and says, "I do know you, Lily. I know that you intrigue me and I've never met anyone like you. You make me laugh and surprise me in a good way."

"Really?" My voice is weak to my own ears and he nods. "I've never met anyone like you and when you left, I missed you terribly. I wanted to see you again but felt a little like a kid with his first crush, so I did what I'm good at."

"What's that?"

"Subterfuge."

He shakes his head and says sternly, "Anyway, we should be heading off to eat. I don't know about you, but I'm so hungry I can't function properly. Come on, let's see if French food is all it's cracked up to be."

Leaving me with many questions burning inside, he exits the car and comes to open my door, helping me out like the true gentleman he said he is.

217

As we head into the warm, cosy bistro, our conversation has stirred up many more questions, but I can't help carrying with me a warm feeling inside. Finn has gone to so much trouble for me and who cannot be flattered by that.

Over dinner we talk about normal things. I discover we have the same taste in music and like the same type of films. He makes me laugh and it appears I do the same to him and as the food and wine settles any nerves I may have; I thoroughly enjoy the evening spent with my delicious new friend.

We are both reluctant to leave the comfort of the bistro, but the day has taken its toll and I find myself yawning loudly. Covering my mouth with my hand, I feel my face burning as Finn laughs. "No stamina."

"Yes, I do."

"Not really, but that's ok. I'll settle up and we can head back."

"I'll settle up, you don't get to make all the decisions. Maybe I want to pay."

"You're so stubborn. If it's that important to you, you can pay next time."

"What about this time?"

"I called it, so I'm paying."

He heads off to pay and I laugh to myself. It's becoming a bit of a sport annoying him, and I quite enjoy our exchanges. I suppose I do it to disguise the real feelings that are developing for the man who haunts my dreams at night and appears to be on my mind every waking hour of the day. Is it possible to fall this fast and this hard for a man I hardly know? As I watch him leaning on the bar talking to the barman, I feel a little flutter in my heart and know my answer. Yes, it is because I appear to have fallen hook line and sinker for the impossible man before me. Now I just have to hope he feels the same.

We step outside in the night sky and the stars twinkle above us. I shiver a little as the frost catches me and enjoy the fact that Finn puts a strong arm around my shoulders and pulls me close. "You see that star, Lily, the one furthest to the right."

I peer up and see a star apparently on its own, twinkling a little brighter than the others.

"What about it?"

He says huskily, "That's a very special star because it's the star of new beginnings."

"You're making that up."

Shaking his head, he pulls me just a little closer. "No, I'm not and do you know how I know?"

"How?" I am mesmerised by the light in his incredibly blue eyes as he stares into mine and suddenly any chill in the air evaporates in a wave of heat that floods through my body. Finn whispers, "Because of this."

He lowers his lips to mine and kisses me so softly and sweetly, it causes butterflies to invade my stomach. Unlike our past kisses, this one is more hesitant, less rushed and a lot more lingering. He doesn't make a move to pull away and just pulls me closer, wrapping me in his arms where I seem at home. Kissing Finn under the star of new beginnings means so much more than before. He has promised me this isn't just a moment in time, but possibly the start of something incredible. Kissing Finn feels like the most natural thing in the world, and I don't question a minute of it. As the star of new beginnings shines down on us, I don't even care if he's making it up. The fact he mentioned it at all gives this kiss greater meaning, and I'm in no hurry to finish what we have just started.

♥28

When I wake the next day, it's in Finn's bed. As I stretch out in contentment, I wonder if he slept half as well as I did.

True to his word, he swapped rooms with me and although we did kiss some more when we returned home, that was all we did. I am happy to take things slowly because I don't feel in any hurry to move this relationship, if that's what this is, on any faster. If, as I believe, we have a lifetime together, the rest will come when it's the right time.

Once I'm ready, I head out to the kitchen and see that it's empty. There's a warm pot of coffee on the range, and so I know Finn is up already. I hear the shower running and smile to myself as his attempt at singing drifts through the small cottage.

As I pour myself a coffee, I almost have to pinch myself. This is amazing, I never thought I would be so happy in such a basic environment. I'm used to all the mod cons modern living dishes out and I love my material possessions and such luxuries as hot and cold running water and heating that actually works. However, it appears that I can stand the most basic of conditions if Finn is by my side because ever since I've met him, we have struggled against adversity.

He interrupts my thoughts by heading into the room dressed only in a towel slung around his waist and my mouth goes dry. Wow!

221

Seeing Finn almost naked is a fantasy come true. As I thought, he has an extremely muscular body which is decorated with some very interesting tattoos. He is clean shaven and strangely tanned for winter and as I openly stare, I see a small scar running across his abdomen and he says lightly, "Appendix."

Blinking, I look up into his amused face and he points to the scar, "I had it removed last year. It was quite aggressive and I was in hospital for a week with this one."

Feeling a little ashamed that he caught me staring, I quickly pour him a coffee and say with a squeak, "You must be freezing, drink this."

He sits on the kitchen chair and I try to focus on the peeling paint on the wall behind him because seeing him partially naked is too much of a distraction. As he sips his coffee, he says lightly, "You know, we could always tick off one of your items today."

"What items?"

He grins mischievously. "Paint a naked man."

In complete surprise, to my utmost horror, I spit my coffee across the table and look up in shock. "Why would I do that, I've already crossed it off my list?"

"I know, but as you admitted, you didn't actually paint the man, they painted you. Well, now's your chance."

Shaking my head, I fumble for every excuse under the sun. "I don't have the materials, sad but true. Never mind, maybe another time."

"I found these in the cupboard in the bedroom."

He nods towards the window sill, where a sketch book and what appears to be a tub of pens and pencils sits mocking me.

Quickly, I think of an excuse. "Oh no, that's not the same. It says paint a naked man. Never mind, thanks for trying."

Finn laughs softly. "Well, I think you should alter it and *draw* a naked man, you see, Lily, you may have ticked that one off but what about me?"

"You?"

"Yes, we're in this together and maybe it's on my list to pose for an artist naked, are you really going to deny me my wish?"

I start to feel incredibly hot and say weakly, "I couldn't, it wouldn't be right."

"Why not?"

"Because it's rude and just a little intimate. To be honest, I wouldn't know where to look."

I almost think he's given up, but then he says firmly, "No, I insist. I think it will break down any barriers between us, and I'm kind of interested to see how skilful you are. Come on, Lily, where's your sense of adventure? I'm game if you are."

His mocking grin makes my mind up for me. He thinks I'll continue to say no, which gives him the power to mock me still further, so I pretend to think and then say, "Ok."

He looks surprised. "Ok, are you sure?"

"Yes, you're right, Finn, maybe it will break down some barriers. Now you come to mention it, I think it's a fantastic idea. After all, who am I to deny you your wish. So, let me get comfortable and I think you can arrange yourself on the chair by the window. Make sure I can see everything because I am, after all, an experienced model myself. If we're going to do this, then we will do it professionally and properly."

I almost think he'll laugh it off, but then I see the challenge in his eyes as he drops the towel with no words spoken. Resisting the urge to look away immediately, I busy myself with the pens and paper and pretend to be engrossed in setting them up.

I hear Finn scrape the chair over to the window and my heart starts racing critically. I can't believe I'm actually doing this. What on earth was Aunt Daisy thinking when she listed this as an option? I wonder if she ever painted Luca?

Trying hard not to make eye contact with my exuberant model, he shouts, "Ready!"

Feeling the heat travel through me as I struggle to breathe, I glance up and smile. "Great, now quiet please, a maestro is at work."

For a moment, there is silence as we both adjust to this weird situation. As I start to sketch out his outline, it becomes increasingly obvious to me that I can't draw. The outline looks nothing like him, and I feel embarrassed as I realise he will want to see the result.

After a while, he says loudly, "So, how does it feel?"

"What?"

"Drawing me. Have you got over your nerves?"

"What nerves, who said I was nervous? I'm a professional artist who does this all the time."

He laughs, and I allow a small smile to grace my lips. It's fun teasing Finn and I like the fact he gives more than he gets. It makes things interesting, and as I settle into my task, I am astonished to find the embarrassment is lessening by the minute.

I even begin to laugh to myself, as I see the ridiculous drawing emerge from the hand of a novice. Goodness, it looks as if a child drew him, and even a stick man has more perspective than this.

Suddenly, my phone rings and I see it's my mum and look up apologetically. "Sorry, I should get this, it's my mother and I haven't spoken to her since I left, do you mind?"

"Of course not, carry on."

Balancing the phone in one hand, I answer it, "Hi, mum. How's things?"

"Oh, you're alive then. Goodness me, darling, anyone would think you forgot how technology works. For all I knew, you could have been murdered."

Fighting the urge to giggle, I say slowly, "Nobody's getting murdered, mum, quite the contrary. I'm having a great time."

"Ok, what's it like – the Château, I mean? I bet it's amazing, like Versailles."

225

"Don't be ridiculous, it's nothing like Versailles."

Finn laughs softly and I roll my eyes, as mum says with interest. *"So, are you coping with the language? I'm guessing this is one situation you can't google your way out of."*

"I don't need to; I have an interpreter."

"Oh yes, what's she like?"

"He."

"He! A man! Are you seriously telling me you're away in a foreign country alone with a man?"

"Yes."

I'm quite enjoying this conversation because obviously the devil has taken up residence in my better judgement and I can't appear to stop.

Mum shouts, *"David, Lily's with a man in France. What do you think about that?"*

I hear a muffled conversation and giggle again as mum says in a whisper, *"Dad's concerned. We both are. It's Aunt Daisy all over again, this time with the French. Now listen, darling and take this in because you're in a vulnerable state and liable to do things you wouldn't normally."*

"Like what?"

"Well, um, I'm just saying that Mr Bianci's story may have messed with your mind. Now, if this French man asks you to do anything strange, report him to the gendarmes immediately. I've seen it all before. These men prey on young vulnerable girls shrouded in grief and you will succumb to it. Maybe it's best if I join you and help out, after all, we don't

want a repeat performance of Aunt Daisy's tragedy."

"Mum you're so dramatic. Aunt Daisy never had a tragedy, she was just careful. I'm not in the same situation as she was in the slightest, so give me a little credit, will you?"

Suddenly, I hear an ear-splitting scream and mum shouts, *"What's that, Lily, are you ok, what's happening? David, something's happened, I think Lily's been murdered by a French man."*

I look up and see a young girl standing in the doorway covering her eyes with one hand, holding a basket of patisserie in the other. Finn starts laughing as he scrambles for his towel to cover his modesty. Mum is shouting, *"David dial the French police immediately! I'll keep on the line just in case the murderer gives himself away."*

"For goodness' sake, mum, I haven't been murdered. It's a local girl who's just freaked out because there's a naked man in the room."

"Naked man, good god, what sort of place is that with naked men running around willy nilly?"

I start to laugh and the tears roll down my face as mum shrieks, *"David, there's a naked man running around, call the gendarmes immediately."*

"Mum! Stop, please, it's just my interpreter and I was sort of painting him to tick off an item on the bucket list."

"The list! For goodness' sake, Lily, tear it up at once, it will be the death of you."

227

I see Finn saying something to the young girl who peers between her fingers before lowering her hand.

Quickly, I say, "Mum, I've got to go, it appears that the bread delivery has arrived."

I quickly cut the call and stare at Finn in horror, who appears to be finding this whole fiasco very amusing. Turning to the girl holding the basket of patisseries, he says something in French and she smiles shyly at me. "Bonjour, mademoiselle. Je m'appelle Sophie."

"Bonjour Sophie, je m'appelle Lily."

I smile sweetly as Finn takes the basket from her hand and hands her some euros, which she places in her pocket carefully. "Sophie lives in the village and delivers baskets of food orders. I placed a daily bread basket order with her when I arrived."

Smiling like the village idiot, I hiss, "Tell her nothing rude was going on. Tell her we were embracing French culture."

Finn grins and rattles off something in French and Sophie giggles. "What did you say?"

"That you were rather eccentric and liked to paint naked men. I told her you were practicing for an upcoming exhibition in London and not to be afraid."

I just stare at him in disbelief and say faintly, "But this was your idea, not mine. It will be all around the village in no time that a weirdo has taken up residence here."

Finn laughs again and Sophie says something that makes him laugh even harder.

"What did she say?" I smile normally as I say it because Sophie is now openly staring at me with interest.

"She would like to see the drawing, if she's allowed."

Still smiling, I say through gritted teeth, "Tell her no, it's not finished. In fact, nobody can see it, tell her I'm a very private person and nobody sees my Art until it's finished and only the ones that pass my stringent quality tests."

Finn starts speaking with animation and they laugh, leaving me feeling extremely uncomfortable. Then Sophie nods and says politely, "Au revoir, Lily, bonne chance avec le dessin."

She nods to Finn and heads back outside and Finn says with a twinkle in his eye, "She said good luck with the drawing."

"I'm going to need more than luck, it's actually really bad."

"Can I see it?"

"Absolutely not."

"Why, I'm sure it can't be that bad?"

Groaning, I take another look at my 'masterpiece' and giggle. "I think a baby could do better than this. Maybe I should take lessons, it's obviously a technique that is learned rather than a natural talent. Anyway, that went a bit wrong, didn't it? I suppose I had better call my parents back

229

to reassure them that I'm ok before they arrive on my doorstep with Interpol."

"I doubt that."

"Then you don't know my mother."

He shakes his head. "Actually, there is no Interpol team. They don't have actual officers."

I stare at him in surprise. "Since when? Is it because of Brexit, are we banned from that now?"

He starts to laugh. "No, they never did. It's just a government organisation."

"How do you know so much?"

He grins. "I know a lot of useless information. Brilliant if I'm on a quiz team, or crosswords, they are usually good for a man full of useless information."

"Well, that's very nice for you, but it still doesn't keep my mother from heading out here with some form of crack team in tow. I'll give her a call while you put some clothes on. I can't believe the day hasn't even started properly yet and we're already the talk of the town."

Finn heads off and I can hear him laughing, which makes me smile. Yes, life is a lot more interesting with Finley Roberts around and I'm loving every minute of it.

Despite the strange start, we are soon busy doing what we came here for. The builders arrive and Finn spends most of his day organising them and making sure they have everything they need. After making the usual endless cups of coffee, I decide to explore this amazing place and set off with my phone to capture some great shots.

The more time I spend here, the deeper I fall in love with it. It needs a complete overhaul, but even in its dilapidated state, it's pretty impressive. Just walking through the weed-strewn gardens is enough to calm my soul. It's as if we're millions of miles from anywhere, and the chill in the air does nothing to dampen my spirits. All around is glorious space with just nature for company. Some may find it a little isolating, but after the hustle and bustle of London, I love it. I can see why people move to the country because it's so different to the city. Even the air is sharper and purer and nothing seems urgent.

The Château is a jewel in a very tarnished crown. It could be stunning but somehow even in its uncared-for state, its breathless. As I walk around the lake, I see my reflection in the murky water and it strikes me that when you break it down, the only person who walks by your side in life for the entire time, is yourself. Others come and go and enrich it but ultimately, you owe it to yourself to do what's best for you. Nurture your soul and happiness will follow.

"Lily, wait up!"

Turning around, I see Finn waving madly and racing towards me. As I wait for him to catch up, I feel the flutters once again as I see the impressive man heading my way. I wonder what it would be like to walk with Finn just part of the way through my life. He would probably annoy me, but we would have fun, that's guaranteed.

He reaches me and grins. "I wondered where you went. The builders are heading off and I thought we could do something."

"What did you have in mind?"

"We could head into the nearest town and take a look, or go for a walk, it's your choice."

Thinking of the town doesn't seem as appealing as a walk, which surprises me. Normally, I'm raring to get to civilisation and if there are shops, I'm in heaven. However, here it doesn't seem as important to me. Even just the walk around the lake is lifting my spirits much more than any shopping trip I've been on, unless you count the time I attended a sale preview evening at Karen Millen, I was beyond excited about that.

Smiling, I say to my surprise, "Shall we just walk."

Finn nods and falls into step beside me. "You know, I was thinking."

"Steady on Finn, you don't want to over reach yourself."

He rolls his eyes and takes my hand as if it's the most natural thing in the world. "I wondered if you've ever been skiing?"

"No, I haven't." I look at him in surprise because it seems like a very random comment, but he looks quite animated. "There's a place not far from here where we could go. I've made enquiries and we could hire all the equipment we need and head over there tomorrow if you like. I could teach you and it would be a great addition to the bucket list, don't you think?"

"Maybe, maybe not, I mean, I'm a bit clumsy if I'm honest and what if I break something? I've heard so many terrible stories of accidents and everything. Shouldn't I enrol in ski school first rather than just head up the slopes with just a wing and a prayer?"

"No, you'll be fine. I'm a good skier and we can practice on the lower slopes first. I think you'll be amazing, come on, let's go and have some fun."

He looks so excited, I don't have the heart to disappoint him, even though I am dreading the thought of it. Honestly, what on earth is he thinking? I've had zero time to prepare for this and feel a little lightheaded as I think about it.

Finn looks a little concerned. "What's the matter, don't you like the idea?"

"What, skiing, of course, it sounds like fun."

"Then what's bothering you?"

Sighing, I decide to lay it out there. It's pointless keeping it to myself and so I sigh heavily. "It's just

233

I don't like the idea of wearing just any old random stuff. What if I don't like the colour and it clashes with my hair? What if it's old and worn and, god forbid, too big? I'll look a complete mess in somebody else's clothes and who knows who's been in them before. Quite honestly, Finn, I'm hyperventilating at the thought of wearing orange, that would be a disaster."

Finn starts to laugh and I stare at him angrily. "What's so funny?"

"You are. On the one hand, you're up for adventure and not afraid of anything it seems. But no, as it happens wearing hand-me-downs is a step too far even for someone as adventurous as you are. Why don't you just think of them as vintage and customise them, or something?"

"With what?"

He shrugs. "A scarf maybe, or that fur hat you brought with you. You know, you will look amazing, you always do."

I say thoughtfully, "Hmm, you could be right, although I doubt I'll wear a scarf. I have a bad track record with them and it could literally be my downfall."

We walk for a while in silence as I think up ways to rock my vintage ski outfit. After a while, Finn says a little sadly, "You know, I'm really enjoying spending time with you, Lily. I thought I would, but you are such fun to be around. I'll miss this when we have to return home."

For once I don't reply with a smart comment because the thought had crossed my mind already. Trying to be positive, I say lightly, "It will be fine. We'll just have adventures at home instead. I'm sure we could make time for them at the weekends or something, after all, isn't it right that you always make time for the things you enjoy the most?"

Finn is strangely silent which worries me a little and then he says quickly, "Of course, we'll make it work."

There's a slight edge to his voice that rings the alarm bells, and I start to worry. He didn't sound so sure. Maybe he doesn't want to see me when we're at home. Maybe he does have another woman waiting in Kent who he devotes his free time to. Perhaps I'm just a bit of light relief, and he never intended on taking this any further than Provence.

Suddenly, I'm not so sure about his intentions, which pounds my heart like a sledge hammer. As the realisation hits me, I swallow hard. How could I have been so stupid? I'm such an idiot and the word 'fool' was created in my image. I never saw this one coming and now it's here I can't deal with it. I've allowed my stupid heart to run riot and it's done something I should have warned it about from the start. I've fallen for the annoying stranger and now I don't know what on earth I'm going do about it.

♥30

Despite my reservations, I actually love skiing. The fact we haven't even made it out of the hire shop yet is of no consequence.

"You look amazing but we really should be going now."

Finn looks like a desperate man, which is nothing to how the assistant looks. All around me is a sea of discarded ski suits, which is a great image for Instagram. Suits of all the colours of the rainbow are piled high and as I look at myself in the mirror, I congratulate myself on a job well done because I look as if I've done this a million times before.

I managed to find an all-white ski suit which will look amazing against the snow. It has fur edging and silver trim, which makes me feel a bit like a spaceman, with an American flag embroidered on the arm. It fits well and feels nice and cosy. I am wearing my amazing fur hat and the ski boots I wore camping, although I think we're picking up some proper ski boots along with our skis. My mirror sunglasses will top this look off perfectly and I cannot wait to get some great shots of me all suited and booted for my, 'living my best life' Instagram story.

As I follow Finn outside, I admire him from under my lashes. He is looking so cool in an all-black ski suit and makes my mouth water every time I look at him. He is so… manly. Sort of rugged and outdoorsy and looks as if he could wrestle bears should the need arise.

I am feeling quite good about myself and follow him outside into the crisp, snowy air, with a renewed energy. I now know why skiing is so popular, it's cool in every way.

We make the short journey to the nursery slopes and Finn patiently tries to explain how things work. It's harder than it looks, and I lose count of how many times I fall over in the powdery white snow. However, he is always on hand with a strong capable arm to pull me up and dust me off, and as the sun beats down from the clear blue-sky, London seems a million miles away.

We mess around on the nursery slope for most of the morning and then Finn says a little wearily, "Shall we grab some lunch and then maybe progress to the next stage?"

"Great, I am feeling rather hungry as it happens."

We head to an amazing looking restaurant that overlooks the slopes and take a seat on the balcony near the edge. Finn laughs as I look around in wonder. "Impressive, isn't it?"

"It certainly is. I never thought being out in the cold light of day would be so magical."

"I know, it makes you feel alive, doesn't it?"

He smiles, and once again my heart beats a little faster. Finn is an incredibly good-looking man, and I still have to pinch myself that he's here with me at all. Added to that, he's good company, so I need to find out what his flaws are immediately because nobody could be this perfect.

We order two glasses of mulled wine and some warm soup with crusty bread, and as the waiter heads off, Finn leans back and groans. "I'm going to miss this when I head back to work."

My ears prick up because this could be my chance to discover what he does for a living, so I say nonchalantly, "When do you have to get back?"

"Another week but I'm dreading it already."

I nod in agreement because despite the fact I'm set on returning to my new role, it has lost a little of its shine since I met him. In fact, it's the last thing I want to do, which surprises me and I know it's because I'm enjoying myself so much with Finn.

"What are you thinking?"

His question brings me back to the conversation and I shrug. "Same as you probably. I'm dreading going back, which has surprised me."

"Why?"

"Because I have finally got everything I want. The fantastic job of my dreams and my life is heading places. With the job will come more money, which means I can probably afford to upgrade my living accommodation and start to enjoy life."

"Are you sure about that?"

I look at him in surprise. "Of course, my pay will nearly double and I know of a great development that's much better than mine where the rent isn't too bad for London."

He shakes his head. "No, not the upgrade. I mean, have you finally got everything you want because I know I haven't?"

As I think about it, I can see he's right to ask and sigh. "On the face of it I have. All I ever wanted was to be successful like my Aunt Daisy. She seemed to have it all worked out, and I thought she was happy with her life. I believed that success brought happiness and that once you had it everything else would slot into place. But…"

I break off and look at the view and notice the strangest thing. A small child is laughing as they throw snowballs at their brother or sister, I can't tell from this distance. However, their laughter carries across the space reminding me when life was a lot simpler. Their parents are taking photographs and laughing too, and as the sun beats down and reflects off the crisp white snow, I feel empty inside.

Images of London in winter cloud my mind. The dark, dismal days are mainly filled with rain and depression. The commute to work, along with half the population, to an imposing building in the heart of one of the busiest cities in the world seems tiresome. Endless hordes of people that fill the day, from the train journey in, to the walk from the tube, crowd my personal space. Then there's the noise from the traffic as I weave my way through the dusty streets that are home to the homeless who seek shelter in the brightly lit shop doorways as most people walk by with not a second glance. It seems a million miles away from the simplicity this

239

day has brought. Deadlines, meetings and pressure used to drive me to succeed. However, the thought of returning to such a pressure cooker is causing me sadness, and as I look at Finn, I see the same misery reflected back at me.

He reaches out and takes my hand and says sadly, "Next week I'm leaving for Berlin. I'll be away for weeks, not really knowing when I'll be back."

I make to speak, but he shakes his head. "Don't ask because I can't tell you. However, I can tell you, I don't want to go. Like you, I've always been a slave to my profession. It excites me and the thought of doing a normal job used to fill me with fear. I love the uncertainty of what I do. The lack of routine and the excitement it gives me. I like the fact I travel and see places nobody normal would ever think of going. I love my life, at least that's what I keep on telling myself, but now everything's changed."

"How?"

"Not how, why?"

"Why?"

He laughs at my confusion and smiles so sweetly I forget to breathe. His startling blue eyes twinkle in the most handsome face I have ever seen. He is looking at me with such a soft look it melts me inside and he could ask me anything right now and the answer would be yes. It probably always will be because I am fast realising that Finn is something good in my life and I would be a fool to mess this up.

"It's changed because of you, Adams. When you showed up in the New Forest with your wheelie case and determination to do things your way, my head has been scrambled. The more I heard, the more I liked you and even that crazy list of yours sparked something inside me that wasn't there before."

Raising my hand to his lips, he kisses it softly and says, "You made me feel something I never have before. I wanted to spend time with you because you made me question the direction I was heading in my own life. Sitting around that camp fire discussing your plans, made me look at my own and they didn't seem so exciting anymore. You see, Lily, when I'm with you - around you, I feel alive. When I'm not, it feels as if something is missing and I don't like it."

My heart is beating so fast I may need an air ambulance, but I would even tell that to wait a minute because every word that spills from Finn's lips is seized upon and held tightly as if it's the finest treasure. Then I watch the light fade and he says sadly, "Life really sucks sometimes."

He pulls away and stares out across the snowy scene, and my heart feels heavy as I see him battling with something. The food arrives which breaks the spell and I wonder what he's thinking because I know what appears to be at the forefront of my own mind – I don't want this to end. I don't want him to head off with no return date. I don't want to go back to my old life without him in it and I don't actually want my old life, even though it's technically a new life in the making.

Thinking of the crumbling Château not a million miles away, I feel a tug on my heartstrings as I realise it's just a temporary place to stay. Soon we will pack up and return to normality, and the excitement of the past few days will be just a delicious memory to think about on the train journey to work, or when the lights go out at night. Real life will interfere and crowd around the memory of when life was simple and there were no responsibilities.

As the tears build behind my eyes, I discover that unlike Aunt Daisy, I would ditch my plans in a heartbeat. If only he would ask me.

♥ *31*

When I wake the next morning, it's with a mind crowded with memories. After lunch we headed off for a mammoth snowball fight like the children we watched so avidly. We skied and I discovered a new passion as I felt the thrill of speeding through the powdery white snow beside a man who is fast becoming everything to me. Then we ate in a romantic bistro overlooking the mountains, and as the candle flickered between us, I fell in love with Finn a little more.

By the time we returned to the Château, I knew in my heart I had everything I wanted in life holding my hand so tenderly.

Last night we kissed and it was different from before. More serious with extra feeling, yet with a desperation that is becoming increasingly obvious. Soon those kisses will be goodbye kisses and the magic will be broken. Real life will interfere and cast its shadow over the magic we have created. We will go our separate ways and just have the photos to remind of us of when life was perfect in a very imperfect world. Our surroundings were far from perfection but at the same time couldn't be more so. Inside is a raging torrent of conflicted emotions, and the whole thing is making me feel so emotional. I don't want this to end – *us* to end and there is nothing I can do about it.

With a heavy heart, I set about getting washed and dressed for the day, and when I venture into the kitchen; I see Finn working on his iPad.

He looks up and smiles. "Morning gorgeous, I think you caught a bit of a tan from all that fresh air yesterday."

I had noticed my new accessory and smile happily. "Yes, it appeared to agree with me. Maybe my skin was shocked at receiving some actual fresh air and sunshine, it absorbed it quickly like a greedy kid in a sweetshop."

Shaking his head, he snaps his iPad closed. "You're a strange one, Lily"

"Says you."

I grin and he pours me a mug of coffee. "So, what shall we do today?"

I sit beside him at the table and sip my coffee thoughtfully. "Maybe we should head to the town. I would love to see the little shops and we could do with a few supplies."

Smiling sweetly, he salutes. "Your wish is my command. As soon as the builders arrive and I've made sure they have everything, we can go."

The sound of the lorries arriving, remind us we are here to do a job and Finn jumps up. "Speak of the devil, I won't be long."

He heads off, leaving me feeling unsettled. After our conversation yesterday, things seem a little forced now. It's as if we are just waiting for this to end and can't enjoy ourselves knowing that we only have a few more days left.

My phone buzzes with a notification and I pounce on it eagerly. Maybe I just need to get back to normal and these feelings will pass.

It's a message from Heidi and I laugh at the picture she's sent of her and Thomas taken on what appears to be a beach in paradise.

"Hey, babe, just checking in with my bestie. Look at my view; I'm guessing you're a little jealous right now. Anyway, I have news and you are not going to believe this. Thomas and I have decided we aren't coming home. Well, we are coming home but only so we can sort things out and pack for an around the world adventure. I know you won't believe it but this trip has changed our lives and now we want more. I hope things are going well with you and the gorgeous Finn. Who knew there was more to life than knitting? Speak soon, we're back next week and can catch up then. xoxo"

Heidi's message has unnerved me. What's going on? Suddenly, life is changing at a break-neck speed and I can't cope. It's not as if I have many friends, and it looks as if I'm about to lose my best one. I'm feeling so low right now because it appears that everyone is doing amazing life-changing things and leaving me behind.

Then again, I have everything I always wanted – don't I? Editor- in-chief of a successful magazine is nothing to be sneezed at and surely many would kill to be in my position – Joseph Maltravers for one.

No, life is changing for all of us and this is just a shift onto bigger and better things – isn't it?

Finn heads back not long after he left and smiles. "Done, let's get out of here before they find anything else to complain about. I need some Lily time now."

He grins, and then I see the concern in his eyes as I struggle to look excited. Heading across, he lifts my face to his and says softly, "What's up?"

Struggling to shake it off, I laugh nervously. "It's nothing, just me being a little selfish."

"In what way?"

"It's my friend Heidi." I sigh and say with a little break to my voice. "She's found true love and is taking it around the world."

I have to laugh at the confusion on his face and lean against him, loving the way his arms automatically close around me.

"She met that guy at the masked ball, Thomas, remember?"

He nods. "Vaguely, I had other more important things on my mind."

Snuggling into him, I sigh again. "Well, they've fallen madly in love and are now off to see the world together. I suppose I'm being selfish and just thinking about what that means for me and not her. Does that make me a bad friend?"

"No."

"You sound so certain but I'm not so sure."

He squeezes me a little tighter. "It's natural. You'll miss her and if you weren't bothered, I'd be more concerned."

"You're a wise man, Finley Roberts."

"You know it."

He pulls away a little and smiles at me so tenderly it brings tears to my eyes. Looking concerned, he says with a worried voice, "What else?"

"I suppose it's the last straw, really. First Aunt Daisy died and I thought that was the worst thing that could happen."

"Well, death is pretty bad."

"I know but then Sable told me she was leaving."

"And that was worse than your Aunt dying?"

I laugh softly. "Of course not, but in a way, part of my life ended when she told me. You see, I have always feared her a little but have the utmost respect for her. She's ruthless but fair, and I don't think she's ever made a bad decision in her life. I suppose I'm worried I'm not up to the job of filling her shoes. What if I fail? What if the magazine loses readers because of my incompetence? What if I murder Joseph Maltravers because I'm likely to do that within the first hour?"

"Who the hell is Joseph Maltravers?"

"My deputy editor. Sable thinks he's perfect but I'm not so sure."

"Then fire him."

"I doubt it will that easy. No, I'm not really sure I'm ready for this, Finn and added to it all…"

I break off and squeeze my eyes tightly shut to try and stem the tears that are never far away.

"What?" His question hangs in the air and I wish I could bat it away rather than face it but the silence that accompanies it demands an answer. For a moment I hesitate because I'm not sure I want to open up the can of worms that is festering inside my heart but Finn is not a man who backs down easily and he pulls my face to look at his and I see the urgent glint in his eye as he waits for the answer. For a moment, I think of something else to say – anything but the real reason my insides are tied up in knots that will take a miracle to untangle. The concern in his eyes threatens to destroy me and I say almost fearfully, "I don't want to leave you."

As the words make it out into the open, I close my eyes. There I've said it, laid out my foolish heart for him to do with what he will. I'm not sure I dare open them because I might not like what I see, but his voice has such a command to it as he says. "Look at me, Lily."

I open one eye only, as if scared of what I might see, and to my surprise he is grinning like the Joker in Batman. I open the other in surprise as he shakes his head and looks so happy, I wonder if he heard me correctly. Then he pulls me tightly and devours my lips in a kiss so explosive I forget to breathe. He explores every inch of my mouth with his and fists my hair as he ignites a sudden flame of passion inside me that Felicity and James would be proud of. I have never been kissed like this before. It's so primal, so intense and so sexy I'm about to lose my mind.

When I think I already have, Finn pulls away and the look in his eyes makes me hold my breath as he says, "I feel the same. I'm dreading leaving you, and it's been on my mind for several days now. The thought of going back to my usual life is not a pleasant one. I don't know how this has happened, but I have fallen hard for your strange little ways and the annoying way you have of making everything crazy seem normal. You are the person I've been looking for Lily Rose Adams and if you feel the same, we can work it out."

"We can – you do?"

I stare at him in amazement as he laughs. "Love conquers all, doesn't it? Maybe this could work. Who knows, we could find a way out of the madness and grab our happy ever after. It's worth a try, isn't it?"

Nodding like a madwoman, I jump impulsively into his arms and as they wrap around me and my legs wrap around him, we start laughing like crazy people as he runs me right out of the door and around the little courtyard. A passing builder looks at us in complete surprise and shakes his head muttering, "Fous britanniques."

I couldn't care less what he said because all I care about is doing some kind of crazy dance with me in his arms. We can't stop laughing and even the fact it's starting to rain doesn't deter us until I squeal, "Finn stop, I can't believe it."

"What?"

He looks concerned as I start laughing uncontrollably and then start singing at the top of my voice.

♫Rule Britannia!
Britannia rule the waves.
Britons never, never, never shall be slaves.
Rule Britannia!
Britannia rule the waves.
Britons never, never, never shall be slaves. ♫

He looks at me incredulously and I point to the sky.

"Singing in the rain, it's on the list, along with do something spontaneous."

"And you're singing Rule Britannia, are you mad?"

"Yes! Mad for life and bucket lists. Mad for adventure and new beginnings. Mad for France and mad for…"

Breaking off, I say softly, "And mad for you."

This time I kiss him, softly, tenderly and with as much love as I can possibly pour into it because I want him to know how much he means to me.

♥32

"I'm sorry, Lily."

His voice breaks and I battle to keep it together. Smiling bravely, I shrug. "It can't be helped."

As I watch Finley zip up his large bag, it takes all my strength not to break down. He's leaving.

I still can't believe I could go from being the happiest woman in the world to the saddest in twenty-four hours.

I focus on a piece of peeling paint above the door frame and try not to think about what's just happened.

We were going to drive to Monaco today. We were so excited and had it all planned out. I even packed a picnic and was looking forward to a day of creating delicious memories with a man I'm crazy in love with. We were going to look for seashells on the beach and may even have ticked the skinny dipping off the list, although I'm not sorry that one's unlikely to happen, it is January, after all.

Then Finn got the call that burst our bubble. He's got to go. I can't even ask him where because he won't tell me.

"I'm so sorry, darling, this wasn't meant to happen."

Trying to be brave, I say in a dull voice, "It's fine, hopefully you'll be home soon."

The silence answers my questions much more truthfully than words because I know he can't tell me when that will be. All I know is that whatever Finn does for a living doesn't follow the same rules as the rest of us. His job consumes his life and it's only when the job is done, he gets to pick up where he left off.

Ever since the call came through, he changed. Gone is the carefree joker who appeared to exist only to tease me and in its place is a very worried man indeed. Suddenly, he's serious and pre-occupied. The humour has gone, and I can tell that something is weighing heavily on his mind. He won't look me in the eye and I daren't ask for details because I already know he won't tell me any. Maybe this wasn't such a good idea after all; falling in love with a man of mystery because how can I ever really know the man if he won't let me inside?

I follow him dolefully around the little French gîte, as he removes all traces that he was ever here at all. I struggle to find words because they sound empty even as I think them, let alone throw them into the increasingly cold air between us.

"There, all done."

Looking around, Finn appears to scan the room for anything but the look in my eyes and my heart bangs mercilessly inside me, screaming at me for daring to break it in such a foolhardy way.

Looking sad, he takes my hands and looks so lost the tears escape and my lip starts to tremble. The pain in his eyes is too difficult to see as he says huskily, "Look after yourself until I can return and do it for you."

I nod and he pulls me tightly against him and I don't feel as if I can breathe. Disappointment and fear choke me inside as I face the fact he may not be coming back. Don't ask me why I think that, I just do. It's as if my mind has a sixth sense where he's concerned and something is telling me this is final.

No words pass between us as Finlay kisses me with the desperation of a dying man's last wish. My heart breaks and the pain is intense and I know that feeling will sit festering inside me until he returns to take it away. I can't deal with this, it's too hard and it's as if he feels the same because he pulls roughly away and says tightly, "I've got to go. I'll be in touch as soon as I can."

I watch him head to the door without a backward glance.

I watch the door close softly behind him.

I watch his shadow pass the window and hear the slamming of the car door.

Then I hear the engine start and listen hard until the only sound I hear is the sound of my heart shattering on the cold flagstones beneath my feet.

He's gone, and I never even told him I loved him.

33

I smile at the pretty girl who is washing her hands as I venture into the washroom. She looks slightly nervous and I smile at her reassuringly. "It's Stacey, isn't it?"

She nods and the flush to her cheeks shows me my comment is much appreciated.

"You work in features with Joseph, am I right?"

"Yes." Her voice is nervous, and I wonder when things changed. Why didn't I become that boss I thought I would be? So much for the open-door policy. Ever since I returned from France, minus my heart, I've changed. I started my new job and Sable left, and now it's as if she's never been here. I inherited all her problems and soon found myself floundering in them.

My deputy editor is as arrogant as I always knew he would be and completely rubs me up the wrong way, but Mr Mitchell and Mr Stevens seem to love him. He's always returning from his meetings with them with a triumphant gleam in his eye, showing me he's after my job.

I don't care though. It shocked me to discover that this brave new world I always wanted to conquer is a box with nothing inside. It's all shiny on the outside and promises great things, but when you open the lid, the only thing to be found is disappointment. Is this what drove Aunt Daisy to change direction? Maybe Sable dressed it up to aid her own escape from a life so dull it's a job to drag myself in every day.

As I look at my reflection in the washroom mirror, I almost don't recognise the person staring back at me. Lily Rose Adams, the successful one of the family. Power dresser on a budget and rocking that managerial role as she was always meant to. Perfectly presented to an unforgiving world and outwardly in complete control. What they don't see is the emptiness inside because it's been three months to the day since I left France and still no word from Finn.

I go through the motions and try not to dwell on the time when I was happy. Provence may as well be the moon because it's doubtful I will ever return. Maybe that was my Aunt Daisy moment that will haunt me to my dying day. Maybe I will never find love again and substitute it with money and power to get my kicks another way. Who knows, Finn may well call when I'm in my fifties and tell me he had another wife all the time and now she's left him we can be together. Does history really repeat itself, when one dies it passes to the next in line? It's not something I want to dwell on, so I say brightly, "Are you working on anything good at the moment?"

Stacey's eyes light up, reminding me of my own eagerness for the job not so long ago. "Yes, I've had a great idea for a feature embracing the use of recycling in the home. There are many uses for things we would otherwise send to landfill, and some can even be made into items that would make someone a comfortable living one day. It ticks all the boxes and Joseph said he would see what he could do."

Her enthusiasm brings a smile to my lips and I say warmly, "I will look forward to hearing the details."

She nods and then looks a little uncomfortable, so I smile and make my way into the private cubicle that allows me to shut the world out. Nobody can reach me in here because I am fast learning that being editor-in-chief means that you have to deal with everyone's problems as well as your own.

It's true I now have more money than I ever had before. Three months in and my pay has doubled. If I stay at the job for years, I'll have saved enough to do whatever I want, but then again, what's the point? I don't have anyone to do them with.

Heidi is still away and even her messages don't lift my spirits. All they do is remind me that she's out there experiencing the joys of life with her soul mate. I am not. Mum and dad have gone on a cruise and their photographs also remind me they are living their best life while they can, I am not. Mark has decided to extend his stay in Australia because he is enjoying himself way too much, reminding me that I am not. Even nan and grandad are enjoying themselves because they've moved into the nearest

Maccarthy Stone and have a social life I would kill for. Me, I don't have a social life, I have work.

As usual, I can't hide away in the ladies for long and head back to my desk with a sinking feeling. We are behind on our deadline and I have an afternoon to look forward to where I strike the fear of God into the editorial staff so we can reach our targets.

Sybil is hard at work as usual and is the only thing I inherited that's of any value. She's become just about the only friend I have left, and I think she's getting a little worried about my interest in her social life. I crave every detail because I have none. I want to know where she's been, who with and what she thinks about them. I need to know every detail of her life because mine is so empty. Sable was right, this job is all encompassing. I don't have a minute to spare, and even at the weekends I'm poring over spreadsheets and 'to do' lists. It strikes me that all the fun in my life has gone and nothing is the same anymore.

Sybil smiles when I pass and says lightly, "Would you like a coffee, Lily, I'm heading down there."

Nodding, I reach into my pocket and hand her a ten-pound note. "Thanks, my treat, it's the least I can do if you go and get them."

She smiles her thanks and I think how sad my life has become that the only thing to look forward to is a large latte with full-fat milk. Sable would be disgusted at the amount of caffeine and carbs I consume on a daily basis, but we all have our likes and dislikes and this is the only comfort I have.

Two o'clock comes and Joseph knocks on my glass door loudly and my heart sinks as I see his supercilious smile. "Come in."

He heads in and smirks as he takes his seat opposite me. "Good news oh great one, I've had a fabulous idea for a feature that will make everyone happy."

"Go on."

I resist yawning because just the sound of his voice bores me, but I have to suck it up because the problem I have with him lies with me. If I was being generous, he is actually very proactive and keen to succeed, so I can't fault him on that. However, what I don't like is the stories I hear of him talking down to his staff and reducing them to tears. The word around town is that nobody likes working for him because his remarks are as cutting as any sharp knife and nobody likes that in a person.

"Ok, hold the front page because my idea is bang on trend."

I feel interested as I see the excitement in his eyes and say a little more agreeably, "I can't wait to hear it."

"Well…" he leans forward and says in a hushed voice, "It involves recycling old items into new and giving them new life by applying a few designer touches. As you know, we are Designer Homes - *on a budget,* so what could be better? We showcase ways to reduce landfill and, in some cases, the people have made cottage industries out of their ideas."

I stare at him with a blank expression and say politely, "And you say this was your idea?" he nods, looking smug. "And nobody else helped you?"

Shaking his head, he says emphatically, "Absolutely not, that bunch of airheads can't see past their Instagram feed."

A cold feeling swamps me as I feel like stapling his smug smile to the wall, but I shrug instead and call through to Sybil. "Darling, can you ask Stacey to come in for a minute?"

I relish the colour fading from Joseph's cheeks as I stare at him with a hard look. "What, my Stacey? The little assistant who thinks she's above everyone else."

He stares at me incredulously and says, "What do you want with her, surely anything you have to say should come through me?"

I say nothing and just tap on my computer to make it look as if something important requires my attention, but inside I'm seething. How dare he take Stacey's idea and pass it off as his own. He can't even give her an ounce of credit and is taking it all for himself.

It doesn't take long before Stacey appears at the door, looking as if she'd rather be anywhere but here. I see the frown directed at her by her boss, and she appears scared of me for some reason.

Smiling reassuringly, I point to the spare chair in the corner of the room. "Pull up a chair, Stacey and tell Joseph your idea that you told me in the ladies' restroom."

Now Joseph looks as if he's about to pass out and Stacey repeats what she told me and I hate the fear in her voice as she stutters in her delivery. Then I look at Joseph pointedly, who has the grace to look a little uncomfortable.

Turning to Stacey, I smile. "That's a fantastic idea. When did you say you discussed it with Joseph?"

She glances sideways. "Um... this morning. I thought about it when I saw a programme on the discovery channel last night. Apparently, it's a huge industry in America and people are really embracing it. They compared it to life after the war and the fact that people are rebelling against commercialism to save the planet. It was very interesting and I think it's on catch up if you want to take a look."

"I may do that but if you don't mind, please could you type up an outline and have it on my desk first thing tomorrow? I want to see sample copy and some of your ideas. Contacts, locations that type of thing."

She nods with excitement. "I would love to, thank you for the opportunity."

She looks at Joseph and smiles. "Thank you for putting my idea across, I'm so grateful."

She heads off happily and I look at Joseph sharply. "Well?"

"Well, what? I heard her talking about the damned programme this morning and it was only when I put the idea in her head about the feature, it began to take shape. She may have seen the programme, but it was me who planted the idea in her head, so yes, I take full credit for that."

As I look at him in disbelief, I can tell he actually believes his own lies. He is so desperate to get the glory he's forgotten it needs to be earned first. I'm not sure what to say, so I just point to the door. "Get out."

He looks surprised because I am not normally this rude, but he really rubs me up the wrong way.

"What did you say?" he hisses in shock and I point to the door again. "I said get out and don't come back until you learn some integrity. If I hear one more rumour about the way you treat your staff, I'm firing you on the spot. People like you make me sick. You've only got where you are on the backs of everyone else's ideas and I'm sick of it."

"You can't talk to me like that, I'll report you."

"Do what you like, but you'll only make yourself look bad. Now, get out and think up your own ideas in future and give credit where credit's due. If you don't like how we operate here, maybe you should start looking for another job, somewhere where your talents would be appreciated."

Joseph storms out and slams the door and the rest of the staff look up in surprise. Sybil looks at me with a shocked expression because I have never lost my temper before.

As I feel their scrutiny, I want to scream because being in this glass office is like living in a goldfish bowl.

I stare at my computer screen and only see my misery reflected back at me. This is not what I wanted, I'm not enjoying this responsibility, and the only reason I can think of for my unhappiness is that Finn never came back.

34

Another month passes before I get a call from Sable.

"Lily, Sable here, are you free to talk?"

"Of course, it's good to hear from you."

Standing up, I close my door and sit facing the window. "How are things at the Château, I bet it's amazing?"

"Everything here is fine, which is why I'm calling, really."

"Go on."

I'm intrigued to hear how things have progressed and she says in her no-nonsense way, "I would like to invite you to visit, this weekend if possible. We could discuss a feature in the magazine which we could make a regular column. I was thinking along the lines of a development diary. You know the type of thing, from derelict to designer, what do you think?"

"Sounds good." I can sense the relief across the phone line as she says in a brighter voice, "I knew I could count on you, those people at Grand Designs are so short-sighted."

"What do you mean?" I feel interested because I love watching that programme where they turn a derelict building into an impressive home. "Did they pass on the chance of the television deal?"

I hear the bitterness in her voice as she says coolly, "It didn't work with their schedule.

Honestly, Lily, contacts count for nothing when it comes to the bottom line. Anyway, it's at times like these you see who your friends really are. Now, book your flight and I'll pick you up from the airport. Come and stay for the weekend and bring your best ideas. We are going to make this the best feature Designer Homes - *on a budget*, has ever seen."

She cuts the call before I even have a chance to pass comment, but I'm not surprised. Sable has always been the same, so it's nothing to be annoyed at. Thinking of Sable, I can see why she was so perfect for the job of editor-in-chief. She didn't care if she hurt anyone's feelings and took people to task, even if they didn't deserve it. She was a perfectionist and expected the same from her staff. If she had been here in this office with Joseph, I'm under no illusion his days would be numbered. Sable is the most professional person I know after Aunt Daisy, and if I'm going to be anywhere near as good as them, I have to up my game.

I'm in two minds about going back to the Château. It will stir up some old memories that I still haven't dealt with. The last time I was there, I was happy and in love. Then it changed one night, and it's those memories that are hard to revisit.

However, I am interested to see the progress and if I know Sable, it will be totally transformed.

As I start to clear my 'to do' list, I feel quite excited for the weekend. For the first time in ages, I'm doing something interesting and it will be good to spend time with my mentor again. Maybe she will put my mind at rest and reassure me that my feelings are normal. I'm sure when I return, it will be with renewed vigour and interest for my job. Yes, this trip is a godsend because it's come at a point in my life that's critical. This will set me on the right path, and now I just need to decide what to pack and book my flight.

***

"Lily, over here."

As I pass through customs, I hear my name and look up to see Sable waving madly from the arrival's hall. I smile excitedly because I am so pleased to see her. She looks a little different from how I remember, probably because I am more used to seeing her in power suits and groomed professionally.

The Sable that has come to meet me looks tired and weary and her make-up looks as if she applied it last week. I feel a little shocked because she appears to be wearing denim and a loose-fitting sweatshirt, and I'm amazed to see Nike trainers replacing the Jimmy Choo's on her feet.

I, on the other hand, have dressed as she would expect me to. A smart trouser suit with a white shirt and chiffon scarf, tied at the neck in a chic twist. My long hair is tamed into a stylish ponytail and the oversized sunglasses that are perched on my head are the rewards of being on the VIP list at T.K. Maxx, enabling me to get pre-sale access. My

Michael Kors bag compliments my scarf and the designer perfume I sprayed liberally in Duty Free, follows me wherever I go, spreading Chanel in my wake, causing many admiring looks to be thrown my way.

Sable looks at me with envy in her eyes, and I take a moment to bask it the moment when I am looking way better than her.

"Sable, it's good to see you."

She nods and says curtly, "Come on, the car's parked outside and the ticket's about to run out."

I almost run after her as she strides through the crowds expecting them to move out of her way. I can see old habits die hard and by the looks of it, Sable still expects people to do exactly as she wants them to, me being no exception.

I am slightly surprised to see an old Land Rover waiting and Sable shakes her head. "Sorry about the mode of transport, darling. Things were so muddy and rather bumpy so we invested in this bone shaker. Just as soon as the drive is re-laid, I am trading this in for a Discovery.

As we head the short distance to the Château, she asks me relentless questions about the magazine which I try to answer with enthusiasm even though, as the days go on, I feel less and less enthusiastic about my new role. However, I can paint a pretty picture with words and I'm sure that Sable is none the wiser by the time I finish.

As she pulls into the courtyard of the Château de rêves,

I look at it eagerly, feeling my heart flutter as I remember how happy I was here. I almost can't bring myself to mention Finn because even thinking about him is painful but I can't help myself and say in a rather high, false voice, "Goodness, it seems like ages ago I was here last, um, have you heard from Finn at all?"

"Yes."

If I was hoping for more, I'm to be disappointed because as we park up, Sable says briskly, "Come, I'll show you to the gîte."

Racing to keep up with her, I try to sneak a look at the place that immediately felt like home when we bumped up the dusty driveway. I feel excited as I see the difference a few months have made and the hard, cold, barren ground has been replaced with the delights of spring. Beautiful flowers that must have bloomed here for generations, poke out from every crack in the paving. The borders are no longer bare and twig like as the leaves now cover them in splendour. The sun is shining on what was once a crumbling stone almost ruin and lights up the majestic beauty of what can only be described as a princess castle. The rickety old metal windows have been given a new lease of life and sparkle in the brilliant sunshine, and I gasp in delight. "This place looks amazing; you've done a fabulous job already."

Sable looks around disparagingly and shrugs. "Maybe this bit is ok, but the rest is a disaster. I never thought it would take this long and so much money."

I stare at her in surprise because it really hasn't been that long at all. A few months to transform years of neglect, she's deluded.

However, as I pass the courtyard where Finn and I sang in the rain and hear the birds singing their welcome from the trees, I feel a burst of sudden happiness that I haven't felt since I left. This place is so magical, and Sable doesn't know how lucky she is.

My heart beats furiously as she leads me towards the same little gîte that Finn and I stayed in, and I notice it hasn't changed. It still looks charming with its slightly mismatched appeal, which I'm grateful for. There was a certain charm in the rustic décor and I hope that she has left it intact because when I walk through that door, I want to wrap myself in the time I was at my happiest.

I almost can't look, but when I do, my heart settles. Yes, nothing's changed.

As I follow Sable inside, I am slightly surprised and then utterly shocked, as she slams her car keys on the scrubbed wooden table and bursts into tears.

♥35

For a moment I just stare. This is strange. Sable Evans doesn't cry; she's not like the rest of us. She is cool and in control and nothing ever fazes her. However, this Sable is a different woman. This Sable is, dare I say it – human and after my initial shock, my first thought is to rush across and comfort the formidable woman.

"There, there, don't cry, it can't be that bad, what is it?"

Shaking her head, Sable wipes her tears away angrily with a tissue stuffed up the arm of her sweatshirt.

"It can't be that bad you say, well, I beg to differ."

"Why, what's happened?" My voice shakes as a sudden fear grips my heart like an icy glove. What if it's Finn? What if something's happened to him overseas and she's brought me here to break the news? Maybe there isn't a business opportunity here, just a very personal one. Maybe that's the reason I haven't heard from him, and it isn't that he's been ignoring me or carrying on his life with another woman.

I stare at her with fear twisting my rationality and say breathlessly, "What's happened?"

She sniffs and starts pacing the ancient flagstones as she used to do in the sleek cool office of the magazine.

"What's happened, Lily, is that my life has become unbearable. To be honest, I hate this place. I hate the Château; I hate the loneliness that comes with it and I hate the people. They hate me too, it's obvious."

I make to reassure her and she holds up her hand. "Save your words because I know they do. They don't understand me and can't be bothered to wait for me to show them a google translation on my phone. They look at me as if I'm the village idiot, not a woman of power, and they make life difficult for me in every way. You know, I even heard they made up stories about me in the town, which just goes to show the nature of the people I live among."

"Stories?" I stare at her in shock and she nods. "Yes, stories. Last I heard, I was some kind of pervert who got her kicks from drawing naked men. I ask you, what sort of depraved minds come up with this stuff?"

I feel extremely uncomfortable and say timidly, "Shocking."

Nodding, she carries on pacing. "The Château is boring me to tears because it's so… French and I'm not talking chic here. No, I thought it would be fun doing up what was once an impressive residence, but this place needs bulldozing because with every task we undertake, there are three more things that shout for attention. It needs a complete new heating system, re-wiring and re-building in most parts. I'm telling you, Lily, this place will be the death of me."

She stops to draw breath and I say meekly, "What about Arthur, what does he think?"

She looks angry and I fear her answer as she spits, "He's the lucky one. He gets to return to London on the premise of an urgent meeting or consultation. His trips home are increasingly longer, leaving me here…" she waves her hand around in disgust, "In filth and squalor while he wines and dines in London with all of our friends. When he *is* here, he spends most of his time working on some drawing or another and we never even got to take that trip to Paris he promised me as a treat for my birthday. No, I'm telling you, Lily, this place is the stuff of nightmares, not dreams and you don't know how lucky you are."

Her gaze flicks back to me and I feel the intensity of it as she says with a fierce desperation, "Tell me about the magazine. I want to know every detail. I want to know what you're working on, who's pulling their weight and who is not. What's happening with management and how are you coping? I want to hear it all because I crave the information, Lily. I feel as if I've been starved of the fuel that drives me. The oxygen in my day that makes me survive and the meaning of my life. I want facts, figures and details and don't leave anything out. I want you to brief me on everything because I'm fading fast and need the energy to deal with this mess we've got ourselves into."

I feel like a trembling animal under the watchful eye of a predator. One false move and she will pounce on me and rip me to shreds. I haven't even sat down and she's interrogating me and so I laugh slightly nervously and start telling her everything.

I pay attention to detail because I can see her absorbing every word I speak with a hunger that ensures I keep going. Even the smallest detail is pounced upon, and by the end of it, her eyes are flashing with excitement and interest. Suddenly, Sable is back and I watch in awe as she becomes the woman I remember and feel the power surging towards me like a sonic wave. Feeling like the trainee I once was, I offload my problems, hoping she will make it all better, and as I tell her about Joseph and his subterfuge, her lip curls in derisive rage.

"Hmm, I should have seen that one coming. You know, Lily, he was always an ambitious animal, but I thought under the right guidance and with proper training, he could be the asset that would drive the magazine to greatness. Yes, he needs controlling and whipping into shape and you can't let him get away with anything. Keep him close and watch him like a hawk. Break him down and re-build him in your image. Take no nonsense and lay down the law. Show him who's boss and strip him bare."

I look at her in dismay because the last thing I want is to see him stripped bare, as she puts it. The last man who was stripped bare before me was in this very room and I can't even deal with the pain that memory brings, so I say slightly fearfully, "How?"

Her razor-sharp stare causes me to squirm and she says sharply, "What do you mean, how? You know how? You belittle him and make him feel worthless. You tear apart his ideas and make him feel inconsequential. You delegate him the worst jobs and set him up to fail, and when he fears for his position, you allow him one more chance. He'll be so grateful; he will do anything you say. You see, you need to break a stallion, Lily, to make him magnificent."

I watch in amazement as she strides around the room looking so animated, I can only stare in complete awe. She is thriving on this. She's in her element and I can tell that she is right back in her office as she tears Joseph off a strip in her mind.

Watching Sable is like watching one of the big five. She is a strong and powerful leader of men and understands the game. She is impressive, unrelenting and powerful, which is why the rest of us struggle to rise to her level.

Seeing Sable here, in the slightly tatty gîte, is like seeing a fish out of water. She's in prison and desperate to break free and my heart goes out to her as I recognise the signs that she's unhappy and longing for the time she was happiest. She is unable to let go of the past to see a brighter future and is so unhappy it breaks my heart because even I can see that Sable is self-destructing in an unnatural habitat.

As she stops lecturing me, she draws breath and I see the light once again dancing in her eyes. Looking at her wrist watch, she says quickly, "I have to go, that idiot builder in charge likes to slope off early and I want to be there to prevent that from happening. The slippery little weasel waits until my back is turned and heads off when he should be doing what I pay him for. Wait there and make yourself at home. We have much to discuss and I need a clear head to sort this problem out once and for all."

Without waiting for an answer, she turns on her heel and strides from the room, leaving me feeling slightly shocked behind her. I've forgotten what a powerhouse she is, and she always did leave me feeling as if I'd just been caught in a storm and lucky to survive.

Slumping back in my seat, I struggle to clear my head. Am I really prepared for a weekend of Sable? Suddenly, my problems don't seem that bad because I know by the end of my stay here, she will have pulled apart every decision I've made in her absence and left me feeling even more of a failure than I do already.

Taking a deep breath, I look around me and my eyes fill with tears. Now the images in my mind are different ones because the only thing I see now are images of Finn. He is everywhere all around and the memories swirl around me like a building storm. Will he ever come back to me, or, as I fear, he's gone forever? Only time will tell, but I'm struggling to feel hope because with every day that passes, that hope gets smaller and smaller.

♥36

One day of life with Sable is enough to make me crave returning to London. As expected, she told me exactly what I'd been doing wrong in her absence, which, as it turns out, was most things. Then she created a bullet plan to help me deal with those problems, with cross-referencing and a power point presentation to reinforce the facts.

She showed me around her magnificent estate and where I saw the beauty in the simplest of things, she only saw the work that still needed doing and lamented the way her life had turned out.

The only thing keeping me sane is that Arthur's due to arrive in an hour which should distract her attention from me for five minutes while she tears him off a strip for leaving her here in the first place.

After having shown me around the gardens and outlined her plans for a yurt filled yoga retreat, she lets me off the hook. "Right then, Lily, I need to get ready. Arthur's due in an hour and I need to make myself look respectable."

She lowers her voice. "I can't afford to let my standards slip because I know he's surrounded by all sorts of gorgeous women in London. The last thing I want is him returning to an old hag because the next time he may not be quite so eager to hurry back."

I look at her in surprise because I never thought of Sable as the insecure type. In fact, I always thought she couldn't care less what people think and never for one moment imagined her scared of losing Arthur. He always appears to idolise her and needs to because what man would put up with her moods and personality unless they were madly in love with her?

She strides off muttering under her breath, leaving me to explore the amazing Château on my own.

As I wander around the rooms, I note the progress they've made since I was last here. Some rooms are almost habitable, and I can just picture the amazing décor she has planned and the luxury her guests can expect. Sable's dream is to make this an upmarket boutique hotel, with all the trappings of five-star luxury.

She has reconfigured the rooms to include ensuite facilities and impressive suites to accommodate her discerning guests. I can only imagine what it will be like for them to relax in a roll top bath, sipping champagne, overlooking the landscape gardens. She told me of her plans to host corporate events and develop the vineyard along with luxury days away, including fine dining and musical events.

Sable's dreams, like the woman, are powerful and if anyone can pull this off, Sable and Arthur can.

However, I saw the defeat in her eyes, not the excitement. I saw the pain of a dream shattered without the hope of a replacement. Sable is regretting the choice she made and can't see a way out of it. I'm not sure I can, but it pains me to think all her plans will be discarded and this place will never really come alive again.

Leaning against the window, I press my face to the view. It takes my breath away and as I remember the laughter in this very room that Finn and I shared, a lone tear trickles down the glass and splashes on the sill beneath.

"Te he extrañado bella dama."

I freeze on the spot as a voice interrupts my thoughts. I don't recognise the words, but I recognise who said them.

Spinning around, I just stare in amazement at the person who has never been far from my thoughts since he left that day and this time the solitary tear is joined by happy ones as I break away and run into those arms I've craved for so long.

As they fold around me, I weep with relief because standing holding me so tightly in his arms, is the man I love, Finn.

For a moment, he holds me tightly and I squeeze him just as hard. There are no words because they don't matter. All that matters is that Finley's back and my heart is so full I couldn't feel any happier.

He strokes my hair lovingly and whispers, "Translated, that means, I missed you, beautiful lady."

My voice shakes as I whisper, "I thought you weren't coming back."

He pulls back a little and the twinkle in his amazing blue eyes tells me he still feels the same as he says huskily, "I was always coming back, it just took me a little longer than I wanted it to."

Again, words don't matter because it's more important to share a kiss. In fact, we could just kiss all night long if I have my way because I don't care about anything other than he's here in my arms, which have felt so empty since he left.

After a lot of kissing, he pulls back and says softly, "I missed you so much. You were the only thing keeping me going and it was the thought of this moment that got me through."

"Through what, Finn, please, you need to tell me for my own sanity?"

He pulls me close again and whispers, "I'll tell you everything."

He takes my hand and pulls me over to the window and onto the stone window ledge overlooking the magnificent landscape. We are sitting in one of the four turreted rooms and it's as if time has stood still. There is no furniture and no decoration. We could be from any era, and that's what's so romantic about this moment. Two people with so much love in their heart about to reach an understanding.

Finn looks at me and I gasp at the tortured look in his eyes. "I could never discuss my occupation because I signed the official secrets act. However, I can tell you a little about it now because I left my job today."

I stare at him in shock and he smiles reassuringly. "I've been thinking about it for a while now and when I met you, it reinforced the fact I couldn't continue."

"Why?" My voice comes out in a whisper and he squeezes my hand.

"Because it's a job for a single man with no ties. I always loved it but as I grew older, I realised I wanted more. I wanted to fall in love and share my life with someone special. Marry, have kids, you know, the full works."

"Why couldn't you do both?"

"Because of what I did. No man worth any value would subject his family to the uncertainty it brings. I would never be able to discuss it and disappear for months on end. I may not make it back at all, and that's why most of the guys are single. It would be selfish not to be."

"Oh my god, Finn, are you James Bond?"

Throwing his head back, he laughs loudly and I stare at him in wonder. He's really here. I can't believe he is. Maybe I'm hallucinating because this all so random.

Shaking his head, he says softly, "Not really, but along those lines. I work for the Special Air Service (SAS)."

I stare at him in shock as he carries on. "Our unit undertakes a number of roles, including covert reconnaissance, counter-terrorism, direct action and hostage rescue. We are a secret team of guys who take on demanding operations. It's not glamorous and it's not much fun but we get to travel the world, albeit undercover and usually to places not in your standard travel brochure."

"But…" I shake my head in amazement and stutter, "But, isn't that dangerous?"

He nods. "Extremely, but we are trained in most situations and work as a team and back each other up."

I can't get my head around what he's just told me. He's a fighter, a man of courage and bravery.

As I look at him, I see him in a different light. He looks tired, and I see the storm of many bad memories in his eyes. He looks weary and jaded and I can tell he's lost weight and my heart aches for the torment he must have gone through over the past few months.

I make to speak, but he places his finger over my lips and smiles gently. "That's all you need to know, Adams. Now you know where I've been and why I couldn't get in touch. However, that's all in my past now because that was my last operation. As of today, I'm a civilian and nobody is happier about that than me."

"You're wrong."

"Explain."

I take his hand and raise it to my lips and kiss it softly before saying, "I'm far happier because I've got you back in one piece and sitting with me now. Nobody could be happier than I am right now and it's because of you."

Just for a moment, we stare at each other with stupid grins on our faces. Then almost at the same time, we shift closer and are soon in each other's arms, kissing, laughing, grinning and generally doing anything at all that requires some form of contact with the other.

Life began for Finn and I that day. No more secrets and no more extended time apart. Finley and Lily did reach an understanding in that room and it proves that dreams can come true and that life can be amazing if you step outside your comfort zone and take a chance on something incredible.

Epilogue

"Hurry up, Finn, they're here."

I tap my foot impatiently because I've been planning this moment for the last year. Trust Finn to mess up the big welcome and I yell again, "Finley, drop whatever you're doing and get here now."

"Stop shouting, you'll wake the locals who are probably enjoying a siesta right about now."

He slips his arm around my waist and pulls me tightly against him, whispering, "I wish we were having a siesta, although I doubt we'd be sleeping."

Batting his hand away, I take some deep, calming breaths and readjust my mind that's always scrambled when he's near.

"There will be plenty of time for that later. This all needs to be perfect, and I can't believe there's a cloud in the sky. That is so inconvenient."

Finn laughs and rolls his eyes. "One cloud in the sky and it's the end of your world. The fact there's also blue sky and sunshine is obviously not good enough."

I can't help but grin and he smiles softly. "It will all be fine; you know we've thought of everything."

Nodding, I lean against him as has become the norm for the last three years. In fact, I can't even remember a time when he wasn't by my side. As mum always told me, he's the left to my right. The

282

salt to my pepper and I'm happy to say I was able to tick several items off Aunt Daisy's list with him. Fall in love, find my soulmate, be happy, all came true when Finn came back into my life.

As we stand waiting for our guests to arrive, he says softly, "Do you regret anything?"

"Of course not, do you?"

"No, but I had already made my decision when I came back. You had a lot more to choose between and I hope that you never regret your choice."

Snuggling up to him, I say emphatically, "How could I regret choosing *us* Finn? There was never any choice to make. As soon the seed was sown, it took immediate root. I have never looked back, unlike Sable all those years ago."

Finn nods, and I can tell he's also thinking of what happened next.

When Sable and Arthur put their proposition to us, it was a total shock at first, but over the next few days we began to see the sense in it. Sable and Arthur would return to London and Sable would take back her job as editor-in-chief of Designer Homes - *on a budget*. In turn, Finn and I would remain in Provence and they would pay us to oversee the renovation of the Château. To be honest, we couldn't have been more eager and as the months went by, we fell completely head over heels with the place, as well as each other.

Then Finn sold his house in Kent and I... well, let's just say I became a woman of means after Aunt Daisy's estate was divided between the family. We pooled our resources and bought a large share of what is proving to be a solid investment.

Château de rêves, or castle of dreams, is set for a bright future, as the hard work of the last three years is about to pay off. It's ready for business and opens its doors to the paying public exactly three weeks to the day.

Finn's hand slips into mine, as we hear the sound of vehicles crunching along the newly laid gravel drive. "You've made me so happy, Lily. I just wanted to tell you that before you start ordering me around like a drill sergeant."

He winks and I roll my eyes. "You love it, it reminds you of your former life."

Finn grins and my heart beats just a little faster as I think about how different our lives could have been. If anything had happened to him in the line of duty, I would never have found such happiness. I believe that everything happens for a reason and the letter I found in Aunt Daisy's dressing room that day set me on my path to my own future.

Where she never followed her heart and let life interfere with destiny, I learned that love was the most important gift you can ever receive and without it, the rest is meaningless.

As I glance over at the bank of daisies that we planted in her honour, I smile and offer a silent prayer of thanks to the woman who always did mean everything to me. We trod the same path, but when it forked, we chose a different route. Without her to show me the way, I wouldn't be here now and I will be eternally grateful to her.

"Penny for your thoughts?"

Finn looks at me with concern and I smile. "I was just thinking of Aunt Daisy and how things could have been so different. I owe this all to her, really."

Finn nods. "She would have been so proud of you."

"Yes, I think she would."

The minibus stops and the guests start to spill out and my eyes mist over as I see the people that mean everything to me – my family and friends. Yes, in three weeks' time we open the doors to the Castle of Dreams, where many weddings and social events are already booked. However, the first one is very close to our hearts because in a few days, Finn and I will marry in this amazing place that we now call home. The people crowding out of the bus are the people we love the most, and yet there is one important person missing.

With a slight break in my voice, I say, "It's a shame Aunt Daisy couldn't be here. She would have loved to help me design the Château."

Finn pulls me tightly by his side and whispers, "She's here, Lily, she always will be because she's held safe in your heart. Every time you think of her she will be on hand."

"How did I get so lucky to find you?"

"Keep telling yourself that darlin' because I'm guessing you are going to have your patience sorely tested over the next few days."

We share a grin and I roll my eyes as I spy mum arguing with the driver and laugh softly. "You know, I wouldn't have it any other way. How can I possibly complain when all the people I love most are surrounding me at a time that is surely the happiest in any girl's life? You know, this really is the castle of dreams because mine came true when I met you."

"Keep talking."

He laughs as mum shouts, "Honestly, Lily, the people here drive terribly. For starters, they drive on the wrong side of the road and don't even measure their distance by miles. I'm telling you, we're lucky to be alive."

Finn laughs as I roll my eyes and say with resignation. "Ok, we may as well just get on with it but I'm counting on you to keep me sane until they all leave."

As I walk towards the mother I adore, eager to enjoy every minute I have with her, I do so with a spring in my step and love in my heart. This is my happy ever after and I have absolutely no regrets and I owe it all to Aunt Daisy's letter.

The End

When one story ends another begins. I hope you have fallen in love with these characters as much as I have because I am not leaving their story here. Make sure of your copy by signing up to my newsletter or follow me on social media or Amazon. Carry on reading for the links.

The Wedding at the Castle of Dreams

Thank you for reading Aunt Daisy's letter.

If you liked it, I would love if you could leave me a review, as I must do all my own advertising.

This is the best way to encourage new readers and I appreciate every review I can get. Please also recommend it to your friends, as word of mouth is the best form of advertising. It won't take longer than two minutes of your time, as you only need write one sentence if you want to.

Have you checked out my website? Subscribe to keep updated with any offers or new releases.

sjcrabb.com

Have You read?

sjcrabb.com

Printed in Great Britain
by Amazon